PRETTY THUGS

SA'ID SALAAM

D1596582

Urban Aesop Publications

Email: Saidmsalaam@gmail.com

Cover Designer: Adriane Hall

Editor: Tisha Andrews

DEDICATION

This work and brand is dedicated to the most thugged out woman I know— Diedra Hunter, better known as Ma. My darling mother who sacrificed so much of herself to raise me right. She earned a bachelor's in political science one year, only to turn around and get her masters the next. All while working full-time and dealing with a hardheaded teen named Sa'id Salaam. I could never repay you for all you have done, and still do. This one is for you, mommy. The prettiest thug I know.

CHAPTER ONE

Harlem, New York

Callie

"Yo, Callie. I gotta make a run with KT and Slime," Voodoo called from the living room.

"Boy, I can't hear you! Come here!" Callie lied and took her position just like a spider does in its web.

"I said..." Voodoo was trying to say but lost track of everything including his name when he saw the trap she set. Nothing elaborate, no pulleys or springs. Just face down, ass up with the perfect arch in her back. Voodoo's head just shook since he knew he was going to be late.

"Said what?" she dared as he undid his belt buckle and let his heavy jeans fall to the floor. It would have been an act of pure ingratitude to look at a picture perfect pussy and not give it a kiss.

Voodoo was a lot of things but ungrateful was not one of them. He scooted her whole body back on the bed and leaned in for a lick. Callie's whole body shuddered just from the touch of his tongue. Her lips blossomed like puckering up for a kiss, so he kissed them again.

"Ssss!" she hissed when his tongue began to twirl. Sorta like a Kansas twister touching down in a trailer park. He said some shit too but his tongue was buried in her box so she couldn't make it out. He did make her cum though, so fuck whatever he was saying.

"Un-uh!" Voodoo laughed when she tried to collapse on the bed. He held up waist with one hand and used the other to guide the dick where it needed to be. That got another hiss from Callie, but it couldn't be heard over the splashing from the deep strokes.

"Don't look down!" Voodoo warned himself like people say when they're on the ledge of a building. Except he was on the edge of busting a quick nut. He tried to think of baseball until he made the mistake of looking down anyway. Seeing himself covered in creamy goodness was more than he could take.

"Give it to me!" Callie shouted when he plunged to the bottom of her box and let loose the juice. Her eyes went to the birth control pack on the nightstand in a comforting glance. He would one day be the father of her children; it just wouldn't be nine months from now.

"You got it!" he shot back as he shot up the box like opps on an enemy block. Busting your gun doesn't feel quite as good as busting a nut though. Close, just not quite. Still enough to make him collapse on her back, sending them both to the mattress.

"Mmmm," Callie moaned when her man gathered her up in his arms like Linus does his blanket. She was his comfort, and he was hers.

"I still have to jet out for a second, ma," he reiterated, but she noticed he hadn't moved. That's how she knew he had to, not wanted to.

"Handle your business. The sooner you do, the sooner we can move to Atlanta!" she cheered. Twenty years of the crime, grime and slime of New York City was more than enough. Especially the slime.

"Hell yeah," he eagerly agreed and reluctantly pulled out of her. It had taken the Harlem native two years to get him to agree to the move. He was a dope boy and didn't know anything but the streets. Those same streets had claimed enough friends and family to change his mind.

Voodoo now ran the crew he ran with his whole life. By default, since the last three leaders ahead of him had lost their lives. The two before them got life sentences for various street shit. He may not have been the sharpest knife in the drawer, but his woman sure was. He was smart enough to listen to his woman, which made him plenty smart after all.

Callie never knew either of the people who produced her. She managed to maintain her sanity and virginity through a slew of foster homes. She met Voodoo at city college even though she was the only one who attended. He was dropping off weed to a customer when he spotted the chocolate chip dipped in dollar store clothes that looked a lot more expensive on her.

He asked to feed her on a day when she was particularly hungry. The small stipend that she got only provided enough for noodles and Debbie cakes. She ate the first steak of her life and gave him the wrong number. He came back and fed her again anyway.

His caramel-colored skin and golden eyes got him all the pussy Callie wasn't giving up for a year. Being her friend when all the other guys just wanted to fuck her, finally won her over.

She told him about her plans to move to Atlanta and he offered to take her once he got his money right.

Two years later and his money was almost right. He doubled his workers' pay when he took the wheel of the crew but still managed to put a hundred thousand in the stash. It had been the magic number to start a new life in the new city. All he had to do now was pull himself away from his partners.

"Ayo! Voodoo!" KT called up from the sidewalk to the open window.

"Prolly fucking that fine ass bitch he got!" Slime said way louder than needed since he was standing next to him. "Bitch fine as fuck, yo!"

"Why I gotta be a bitch, tho?" Callie sighed and shook her head as she rolled out of bed. She looked for a shirt to cover some of that fine so she could check Slime about calling her a bitch. If she had a thousand dollars for every fight started by someone calling her a bitch, she could match the hundred grand they had saved. She couldn't stop people from using the word, but she would fight them about it.

"Chill, yo. You know that nigga is slow." Voodoo sighed since he knew she was about to check him. Even he was tired of his stupidity but needed him on the team. Slime more than made up for his low IQ with his high violence. This was a violent profession in a violent city, so he kept the shooter on his team. "He said you fine, tho!"

"Can't stand you!" Callie laughed and shook her head. "Hurry back and you might get some more..."

"Love you, too, my pretty thug," Voodoo said and pretended to go out the window. He got another laugh out of her before turning to leave. Not without the quarter kilo he was going to sell.

"The fuck, fam?" KT asked when Voodoo stepped out of the building.

"He was tapping that fat ass!" Slime laughed like he was ten years younger than he was. Voodoo just tilted his head as if to ask, *'what the fuck is wrong with you'*. Slime didn't know what the fuck was wrong with him, so he lowered his head. That was good enough for Voodoo, so he turned back to KT.

"You talked to them niggas?" he asked and unlocked his SUV. The brief pause was a cause to look up from the lock.

"Huh? Yeah. They ready," Slime said but looked to KT for confirmation.

"Yeah. Told them five Gs since it's better than the shit they been copping," KT nodded and opened the passenger door.

Slime pulled open the back and slid inside. Voodoo disregarded his internal alarm and started the vehicle. The sooner they sold the rest of this work, the sooner he could get on with his life. The thought of a regular life played in stark contrast with what was happening on the Harlem streets he drove on. His name called in the distance brought him back to the present.

"This nigga thinking about that fat ass!" Slime laughed. "We been calling yo name, B!"

"I heard you," he lied. "Just thinking about this move to Atlanta,"

"Bruh, you for real about that shit?" KT snapped from his side. Voodoo had to turn his head to see if he was for real with his attitude.

"Hell yeah! Dead ass! I'm not going out like Rich Porter, Demencio, Smiley, Alpo..." he snapped back, naming a long list of street legends who died in the streets.

"Shit, I am!" Slime said triumphantly. The stars in his eyes twinkled throughout the whole truck.

The sad part was that Voodoo felt him because he felt that same way once upon a time. Life in Harlem was so bleak and so fast, it's hard to see past it. The goal was to get as much money and gold as possible before prison or the morgue. They had never seen anyone make it out otherwise, so they were none the wiser.

Until Callie came along that is. She had never been anywhere but here herself but was an avid Internet traveler. She had virtually been everywhere around the country and globe. Atlanta seemed full of happy, successful, young black people and she wanted in. It took some doing to get Voodoo to see her vision but once he did, he was sold. She had applied for and was accepted to Atlanta college. All she had to do was get there.

"Word is bond, son! I ain't never leaving Harlem!" KT declared. He left out the adjectives 'alive' or 'willingly' but was accurate. The only way he was leaving the block was in a police car or coroner's van.

"Y'all should be happy I'm bouncing! Then y'all got the block!" Voodoo reminded them. It wasn't much of an incentive for natural born followers. These dudes would always be followers in search of a leader.

A rival named Blu made them an offer but it came at a high price. Neither saved anything of what they made. It was fast money, so they spent it even faster. Not that it mattered since Blu didn't want money to move his work on their corners. He named a much higher price than money.

The truck went silent as the trio turned inward with their own thoughts. Atlanta was plan A for Voodoo. He had a good woman who held him down. The wife type, who would bare his kids one day. Meanwhile, KT and Slime mulled over their plan B. They had talked about it a few times as a last resort.

"Do that shit," KT sighed.

"Do what?" Voodoo asked as he stopped at a red light. KT reached down and slid the truck into park while Slime upped the pistol to the back of Voodoo's head. Voodoo saw the danger in the rearview just before the flash that sent him into the afterlife.

"Fuck, B!" KT shouted when the inside of the windshield was splattered in a gruesome pink from his head being turned inside out.

The plan had been to push him out, take the dope and drive back to the block. The mess the gunshot made, made that more work than they could handle. KT grabbed the coke, then dug into the dead man's pockets.

"I want half!" Slime called as they hopped out and ran off towards the train station. They hopped the turnstile despite the handful of bills and bag full of cocaine.

"This ain't shit!" KT groaned when he counted up the couple of bucks. Voodoo didn't carry stacks of cash anymore since he had been in stack mode.

"Split it!" Slime declared because he was a slimy dude.

CHAPTER TWO

"Awe, man." Callie pouted when she awoke at the same window she had fallen asleep at. She hadn't meant to fall asleep since she was waiting for Voodoo to return. She wasn't sure which upset her most, that she had fallen asleep, or him not returning.

She knew he wasn't home before scanning the block for their truck. He would have woken her up if he had come home. He didn't but she still scanned the block anyway. Voodoo was too loyal to be with another chick, so that didn't cross her mind. A rare sighting of a police car gave her comfort. Only two things could have kept him from being here, so she chose jail over death.

"Messing with them knuckle head niggas!" she huffed and shook her head. Atlanta had many perks, but the best was being nine hundred miles away from KT and Slime. Just the thought of how Slime looked at her sent a shiver up her spine.

Callie's head shook once again when she watched both cops jump out of their patrol car. One hit the weed spot while the other ducked into the bodega. She knew neither was there to make an arrest for any one of the illegalities of either place. One came back with a couple sacks of that fruity weed Voodoo loved so much. The other had two cold beers in hand and they were set to patrol the streets of Harlem. No wonder the streets of Harlem were so fucked up if the police were fucked up.

"Shit!" she fussed when she reached the closet. She had no idea how much his bail would be and hoped the few hundred from her purse would spring him. That would save her the trouble of digging money out of the stash.

The ingenious stash spot would keep police or jackers from finding it, but it was a lot of work to get in and out. Callie was Voodoo's girl, and that meant something, so she dressed the part to bail him out in style. She squeezed into a pair of skin tight jeans to show off the fat ass only one man ever got to touch, kiss and spank. Her tight T-shirt set the jeans off just right along with a pair of Air Max since she still had a trace of tomboy in her.

Callie looked up and down the block once more just in case she overlooked the truck. She especially checked in front of Demetria's building since she knew they used to talk before she came along, and they became a couple. A fact the pretty girl liked to remind her of every chance she got.

"You know we used to talk..." Callie mocked and grimaced at the absent woman. She lifted her chin above it and turned to head to the precinct, then stopped dead in her tracks.

KT stepped from the bodega scarfing down a sandwich while smoking a menthol. That was odd but not as odd as him being on the block while her man was locked up. It got odder when he looked up and saw her. He was usually respectful and nodded when they saw each other. This time he quickly averted his eyes and beat it up the block. His untied Timberland boots flopped loudly as he made his hasty escape.

"Mmhm," she hummed after him. She had always told Voodoo those two would snitch on their grannies. This was just more reason to flee this city. Her head lifted a little higher as she marched on.

"Yo, Callie! What's good, ma!" Slime greeted as he slithered up beside her. He even wiggled his limbs like a snake when he approached. His tongue didn't come out, but his eyes sure licked her from head to toe.

"What's good is I'm looking for my man!" she shot back forcefully.

"Who, Voodoo?" he asked but Callie always made it a point not to answer silly questions. He licked his lips like it was sexy and moved on. "Nah, I ain't seen bro since like, nawmean, couple days."

"Oh, okay then!" She nodded like she didn't see him hop into the back seat of their truck a few hours ago. She couldn't lift her chin any higher or she would be looking at the sky. She still spun and marched off from him.

"Ass fat, ma!" he called out as her fat ass shifted down the block and around the corner. She hailed a yellow cab and rode over to the precinct.

Most police precincts are zoos most times of the day. Especially this one at this time of day. The local cops may drink beer and smoke weed but do make plenty of arrests on a Saturday night. That meant friends and family flooding the precinct to claim them before being transferred to Rikers Island.

Four languages rang out over the crying babies and ringing phones. The desk officer handled getting fussed and cussed at with grace. He replied to every 'fuck you' and 'cracker' with thanks and a smile. Callie waited an hour for her turn and approached.

"Victor Walker," she said as he tapped his name into the computer. His head was beginning to shake 'no' when she added, "Driving a black Tahoe?"

"Yeah," she said and sighed as he shook his head.

"License plate, delta, tango, alpha, 234?" he asked with a curious frown. Now it was her head's turn to shake before he could finish since she had no idea what was on the plate. It could have been an Alaska license plate for all she knew. Still, the coincidence was more than they had thus far. "Have a seat. A detective will be right with you."

"Um, okay?" she reluctantly agreed. She had more questions to ask but the next person had already rushed the desk looking for her man. Callie ear hustled from her seat while she waited.

"Ju got my husband? Hector Guzman?" she demanded like she was frustrated with the cop for her husband's frequent arrest.

"You know we do," he said and typed the name in to see what he was charged with this time. "Possession of heroin, again."

"He's going to be sick, papi. Can ju please give him this?" she whispered loudly and slid a loaded syringe across the desk.

"Have a seat," he said and shook his head. Callie wondered why the woman was thanking him when she even knew what came next. A quick call later and a lady cop came out and arrested her too for possession of heroin. A moment later, a detective came out and over to his desk.

"There," the duty officer said and pointed with his head at Callie.

"Good morning," the detective greeted but spoke again before she could reply. "Can you come with me?"

"Um, sure," Callie agreed and had to rush to catch up. She assumed it was bad but not the worse. Voodoo must have sold to an undercover cop and his friends ran off on him. She let out a heavy sigh at having to dig their money out of the stash to free Voodoo. Her head tilted curiously at the sign on the office he just turned into. The Homicide department must mean Voodoo killed someone.

"Have a seat," the detective said and once again spoke before she could sit. He spun his monitor where a picture of the truck was still stuck at a traffic light. "Is this the vehicle your boyfriend drives?"

"Um...yeah?" she answered unsurely. She was sure it was the truck. Just not sure if she was telling on him for something. He tapped the keyboard and pulled up the next picture. This one knocked all the air from her lungs.

"Is this him? Victor Walker?" he asked of the man on the morgue slab. The room did a half spin and she saw the cigarette-stained ceiling just before the lights went out. More than one loved one fainted out that same chair when seeing their dearly departed stretched out. "I'll take that as a yes!"

&

"*Y*ou okay?" a woman asked when Callie blinked awake from the wildest dream.

"Nah, yo!" she whined when she looked around and saw she was in the same room she just dreamt about. If she was really here, then Voodoo was really dead. "Awe, man!"

"Did Victor have any enemies?" the woman asked since

she had taken over the case. Homicide detectives sometimes traded cases like baseball cards.

"Mmph! He hung around with them!" Callie blurted before she could stop herself. Killing people is cool but reporting it is a crime punishable by death.

"Who? What do you mean?" the woman pounced since it looked like she would solve this one rather quickly. "If you know something, you have to tell me!"

"Nah. Ion know nothing," she managed to push past the anger. It was now clear that Slime's lie about not seeing Voodoo was an alibi. The case was already solved, but she wasn't saying shit to the cops.

"Well, if you hear something..." the woman said and handed her a card.

"Yeah," Callie said and tucked the card into her pocket. She didn't even bother reading the name since this same cop might be investigating her soon because she was going to get some get back for Voodoo. He had taught her how to shoot along with many other things. KT and Slime were going to get theirs, and soon.

Voodoo had a mother and brother up in the Bronx, so she headed over to the train. This wasn't the kind of news you shared over the phone. They had just been there a few weeks ago, so the route was fresh in her memory.

New Yorkers don't need GPS or even a street address. If they have been there once, they can get there again. She blanked her mind on the way uptown until they reached 161st street. She walked up a few blocks and over a few more and entered the tenement building.

"Who?" a woman's voice called in response to the knock on the door.

"Me. Uh, Callie. Voodoo's girl?" she replied since she wasn't sure if the woman remembered her name.

"Girl, I heard!" Voodoo's mother said when she pulled the door open. Her eyes were bloodshot red from either crying or the malt liquor on her breath. Nevertheless, she pulled her in for a hug. Perhaps a little too hard since it forced a malt liquor belch from her chest. "Excuse me. girl. Come in."

"Thanks," Callie said and followed her inside. She didn't see the other son and asked, "Where's Capo?"

"He went down to see if he could get Victor's truck from the police. That's how we found out. Mmhm, saw it on the news," she explained but that really didn't explain what Callie was wondering.

"Why?" she asked since it was her and Voodoo's truck in her and Voodoo's names.

"Well, you know. They brothers..." the woman said and took a swig of her beer.

"Oh okay," she replied and stood since she did what she came to do. At least half and Capo could do the rest. He could avenge his brother's death. "Tell Capo to call me, please?"

"Okay, baby. You have a few bucks I can hold?" she asked and stood too. Callie smirked and squeezed a hand into her purse to peel off a few bucks without her seeing the rest. She knew right then she wouldn't be helping to put her son in the ground. Capo was in the streets as well and should be able to help. She would wait for his call.

Callie wasn't surprised to see KT and Slime on the stoop they spent most of their life. They were balling a little more than normal since they were selling the quarter key they took from Voodoo's dead body and keeping the money. A quarter of it was going directly up their noses while another quarter was being sucked up the noses of the local hoes.

Once again, KT diverted his eyes while Slime locked his with her. Callie glared at him as she entered the building. She marched straight inside and straight to where Voodoo kept the gun. She was all the way in the hallway when she remembered she wasn't a killer. She was just a girl, so she went back inside and cried like one.

CHAPTER THREE

"*H*uh?" Callie asked in reply to the knock on the door. People didn't come by the apartment often, and never without calling first. She looked at her phone to see if she missed a call. She hadn't, so she strained to think who could be knocking as they knocked again. She grabbed the pistol she had slept with and stood. Whoever was knocking knocked again as she marched towards the door.

Uh-oh, she thought since only the police knocked like that. She would know since they came knocking once before, before knocking the door down. They didn't find anything then since everything was tucked in the stash. This time she had the gun in her hand. There was no time to put it away, so she stuck it under a sofa cushion and went to the door. "Who!"

"Me!" a male called back. Callie tilted her head and eased up to peep out the peephole.

'The fuck?" she wondered when she saw the familiar face. Familiar enough to unlock the multiple locks and snatch the door open. "Capo? What are—"

"Mommy told me you said to come by," he said and hugged her tightly. Too tight with his whole body pressed against hers. Too long too and made her feel uncomfortable.

"Call. I told her to tell you to call," she corrected him and peeled herself out of the awkward embrace. Just in time before Capo's dick got hard. He looked at her ass and legs in her shorts as she went to sit on the cushion on top of the gun.

"Yeah. No I just wanted to make sure you good," he said to her legs as he sat in the middle of the same sofa.

"Nah, I ain't good! Them niggas killed my man!" she growled ferociously.

"Who!" Capo demanded and hopped to his feet like he was ready to go handle his business right then.

"That nigga Slime! Him and..." she was informing but saw his face change as she spoke. "KT and what?"

"Huh? Oh, nah. I'ma handle that! Just not yet. Gonna rock 'em to sleep. Let 'em think it's all good," he said real fast. Fast enough for her to know he wasn't going to do shit. This nigga was shook.

"Word." She nodded and looked at the door as she mulled over the words to walk him out.

"Oh! We need to get the title 'n shit to get the whip. They said cuz my name ain't on it, you gone hafta..." he rambled like even he knew it was some bullshit. He had called dibs on all his dead brother's belongings before the man was even buried.

"Word. It's at my aunt's house. She'll bring it to the funeral," she said and waited for what never came. He never made the offer, so she made the ask. "Speaking of funerals. You gone help me bury your brother?"

"Who?" Capo asked, even though they were alone. Callie pressed her lips together so the 'fuck nigga' and 'bitch ass nigga' twirling around her head didn't spill out of her mouth.

She knew Voodoo wasn't particularly close to his brother and could see why under the five minutes he had been here. "Oh, okay. Nah, I ain't got no bread right now. You may have to get it and I'll just pay you back."

"Word," she said and nodded and accepted the full weight of putting her man in the ground.

"Oh yeah! Mommy said we should just split the money three ways," he said and nodded along with himself.

"What money?" Callie asked in legit confusion. She was smart enough to have life insurance on her high-risk boyfriend but didn't. Even though carriers didn't cover dope boys since it's such a hazardous profession. Still, she asked, "What money?"

"Shit, bruh was moving major weight!" Capo laughed. He didn't mention the four thousand he owed for the work his brother had just fronted him. He couldn't since he didn't want to use it for the funeral. "I knooooooow y'all sitting on swole!"

Are you fucking crazy! Callie blinked but managed to keep it inside. She had to think quickly since his eyes had finally left her legs and looked around the apartment.

"Ion know where he kept his money at?" she asked like a damsel in distress. "I thought he had y'all moms holding it?"

"Word?" Capo nodded and thought. His mother was just as sheisty as he was, so it could be true. He had to find out, so he took one last look at her legs and stood. "When is the funeral gonna be?"

"Saturday," she guessed. Now that she accepted it was all on her it was time to get it planned.

"See you Saturday," he said and reached for another hug. Callie sneezed in his face and followed up with a coughing spell. It did the trick, and she locked the door tightly behind him.

I need to move, Callie thought to herself. Casually at first until it dawned on her. *Immediately!*

❦

The funeral cost just over ten thousand dollars. Callie managed to scrape that together from Voodoo's pockets and drawers, so she didn't have to dip into the stash. She would soon since that was the last of the cash on hand.

"Hell nah!" she fussed to end the debate about burying Voodoo with his jewelry. She thought someone might dig him up to steal it, but it wouldn't even make it into the ground. The workers at Williams funeral home could strip a body of valuables during the ride from the church to the cemetery. Pry out gold fillings and teeth, cut fingers off for rings right in the back of the herse.

She left it on the dresser and headed over to the church. It dawned on her that this would actually be her first time inside of one. An Uber would have been quicker, but she walked since she was in no hurry to put her man in the grave. She still hadn't picked up the truck yet since it was a crime scene.

"Hey, girl! I'm so sorry about your loss!" Demetria moaned when she saw her.

"Thank you," Callie said and accepted the hug she was offering.

"You know we used to talk back in the day," she reminded her like she always did. She left out the part that they only talked before sex since that's all she had to offer. Lately, she must have been offering it to KT and Slime since she spotted them together a lot. "He loved you, tho!"

"I loved him, too," Callie said and finally broke down right

24

there on the sidewalk. Demetria wrapped her up and held her tight so she could get it all out.

"Okay, ma. Dassit. Straighten yo' crown so we can send Voodoo off like a boss!" Demetria insisted and wiped Callie's tears away.

"Thanks," she said and accepted the help. Her chin lifted and they marched over to the church. Voodoo was loved in these streets, so the streets showed up and showed out.

Mourners mourned in 'Long live Voodoo' shirts as they filed into the church. Most knew Callie and gave her condolences as she made her way up to the front. She spotted Voodoo's mother and brother on the front pew and took a seat.

"He ain't keep no money with me!" his mother relayed immediately.

"Huh?" Callie asked and looked over at the casket. This was why they were here, but she was talking about money.

"She said bruh wasn't keeping his stash with her," Capo was saying but Callie got up and went to her man lying in the box. His mother and brother couldn't even let him be buried in peace without worrying about money.

"I need you more than ever, yo." She sighed and rubbed Voodoo's face. That usually cocked his mouth into a smile, but she got nothing this time. His face was cold and stiff, and she would never see that smile again.

The preacher preached but she tuned him out. She was his best friend in life so no one could tell her anything about him in death. Once he said what he said, the mourners lined up to say parting words to the dearly departed.

Callie finally stepped aside to let them have a last word in private. She took note of every face, but it was the two faces she didn't see that stood out. KT and Slime were noticeably absent. Just more proof they were responsible for Voodoo being on his back in that box.

&

*T*he cemetery was way out in Queens, so only a quarter of the mourners from the church made the trek. Callie made the uncomfortable ride in the family limo with the family. She sat next to Capo since his mother was still trying to talk about money.

"He ain't left no money with me! You got it and you need to share it with us! We his real family!" she finally demanded when Callie wouldn't respond.

She just kept her face out the window and counted down the minutes until she never had to see either of them again. The preacher had some more to say as the casket was being lowered into the ground. Callie missed most of that speech too. Not because she didn't want to hear it, but because Capo was still in her ear.

"Look, I was reading in the bible," Capo said and paused to let that sink in because it was the Bible and all. He expected that to get her attention, but it didn't, so he kept talking. "Yeah so, when a man dies, his brother supposed to marry his wife."

"What?" Callie snapped loud enough to turn heads. Capo was undeterred and kept on with his plan.

"Word, so me and you gone hook up. Can't no one say shit either, cuz it's in the Bible!" he said as she looked at him dumbfounded. That didn't stop him from delivering the rest of his plan. "Yeah, then we can split the money. We ain't gotta give her shit!"

"Uuuugh!" Callie shouted and took off running. She had seen and heard enough treachery for a lifetime in a few hours.

26

The casket hadn't finished its descent but she couldn't take another second of his greedy family.

Callie ran through the graveyard nearly blind from her tears. Her life had been rough going from foster home to foster home. Fighting foster sisters, foster brothers and foster parents. Studying on her own to make up all the classes she missed from all the moves.

She had finally found happiness and it was snatched away from her. She rested against a tombstone and cried until the tears ran out. Not just for now, but for good. When she stood up again, she made a vow not to shed another tear. She wiped her face clean and headed back to the now vacant gravesite for a word with her man.

"I gotta go, B. Gonna finish what we started. Moving to Atlanta. Going to school," she told the fresh dirt. "Don't worry tho, I'll always be your pretty thug!"

CHAPTER FOUR

"*Y*'all time coming!" Callie snarled as she locked eyes with Slime. As usual, KT turned his head when he saw her back on the block. She shook her head at them both for missing the funeral.

It was a long day and all Callie wanted now was a shower and to climb in her bed. The beef patty she ate on the way home would have to do for dinner since she didn't have the energy to even stop in the bodega. She saw the first sign that her day was far from over when she walked into the lobby of her building.

"Huh?" she asked of a lone neon pink sock at the bottom of the stairs. It was just like the ones she got from a foster sister a few foster homes ago. A present she brought back from Puerto Rico, but it couldn't be hers since hers were safely tucked away in her drawer.

Callie stepped right over the sock and headed up the stairs. The long day made the stairs seem higher and steeper, but she managed to make it to her floor. That's where she saw more things that looked like her things on the floor.

"No," she moaned and ran down to where her locked door should be. Instead, it was nearly off the hinges and wide open. The first thing she saw was the large white spot on the wall where a large TV once covered.

Fuck that TV, her mind screamed as she rushed into the bedroom. She didn't notice it too was stripped bare down to the Polo comforter and sheets on the bed. The closet was emptied but she didn't care about the clothes.

She saw the carpet was still in place but couldn't breathe yet. She broke two fingernails as she snatched it out from the corner. The wooden floor planks below were still intact which meant the small fortune beneath them was too. Now she could breathe.

"Would you look at this fuck shit!" Callie growled. Both sides of the "his and her" closet were stripped down to the bar. She looked back down and now noticed her and Voodoo's shoes, sneakers and boots were all gone.

She stepped out and saw the mattress pulled off of the box springs. People who hide money under the mattress don't have much money to hide. The gun that lived there though but was missing as was Voodoo's jewelry she left on the dresser so it wouldn't get stolen.

For real, tho? Callie wondered and let out a chuckle when she pulled the fridge open. Her head shook woefully when she saw it too had been rummaged through. They stole all the food, including leftovers. Whoever hit the fridge must not like frozen brussel sprouts since it was the only box left which was fine since it contained the last eight ounces of coke. Callie grabbed the few things left in the living room and stomped back down to the street.

"Y'all forgot this! Here! Here!" she shouted as she tossed items in the street. It was a good show but most of her stolen items were still in the building.

KT and Slime kicked the door off the hinges and searched for money and drugs. They settled for the jewels and pistol and got out. The neighbors had seen the couple coming with bags and boxes for years, so they went to steal what they could. Word spread and soon the apartment was filled with looters like a riot. First, the neighbors and finally, the junkies came to strip any leftover meat from the bone like vultures.

"Come on, yo," Demetria urged and steered Callie back inside. She walked her back up to the apartment and inside. "Damn! They took err'thing, yo?"

"Even the dirty clothes from the hamper," Callie replied and shook her head. Demetria retrieved a temporary fix and lighter from her purse. Callie only smoked occasionally with Voodoo but accepted the blunt when passed. "KT and Slime did this!"

"Wouldn't doubt it. They selling for Blu now. That nigga got on the block before Voodoo got settled in his casket," she revealed. "You know we used to talk."

"Who?" Callie asked since they were speaking about four different people.

"Allum!" she said and giggled like being a hoe tickled. "I know Blu gonna be mad if he find out them niggas is selling they own sacks along with his!"

"Word," Callie agreed and took another toke. The warm glow of THC spread throughout her body and made her weary. "Thanks, girl."

"No problem. Let me know if you need anything," she said and hugged her before departing.

"Anything? Shit, I need everything!" Callie said, looking around the scarce apartment. It wasn't rape, but the next worse thing. Luckily, sleep swooped in and took her away if only for a few hours.

𐙚

"On God," Callie growled when a steady knocking on the door woke her up.

She looked over to where the pistol would have been, but it was gone. She was still clutching the only weapon she could find before falling asleep. The butter knife was probably only good for toast but it was all she had. Anger still propelled her to the door and snatched it open so she could tell Capo off once and for all. Her mouth was opened but the faces froze her in place.

"Yo, we need that work!" Slime demanded and stepped forward like he was about to barge in.

"Chill, B," KT said, holding him back then turning to her. "We had nine ounces left. We need that."

"Well come in and get it! You know niggas ran up in my shit while I was burying my man. They got that too!" she snarled. The expensive knife set had been stolen, but she would try her luck with the butter knife.

"We ain't see no dope!" Slime protested and confessed until KT jumped in.

"Yeah, niggas was in and out the building with shit. We tried to stop 'em, but..." he said and let the lie hover. Then pulled his partner away before he made a full confession.

"Yeah," Callie said as they rushed off. They hadn't made it to the stairs before a sinister plan popped in her head.

The building superintendent passed them on the steps as he came up to fix the locks. He usually smiled and spoke but not today since he had collected a few of her outfits for his wife. She had no choice but wait him out before setting her plan in motion. First things first, and she headed into the bathroom to bathe.

Voodoo was right about protesting when Callie wanted

designer bath towels since someone stole them all. Her body still needed to be washed, so she bare handed her box and breast with a bar of soap. A half bath will always beat no bath, even when you have to put the same clothes back on.

Callie shook her head at her reflection in the same black dress she wore to the funeral. Then spun and headed out to see if she could go cause a few more funerals. The block was bustling when she stepped outside. A few heads turned in her direction, but she lifted hers and marched away.

She passed the exact same spot the infamous Alpo recently met his fate. A memorial with pictures, flowers, candles and stuffed animals was laid out. A few young thugs in construction Timberlands promptly came through and decimated it. They stomped and kicked the trinkets onto Frederick Douglas Boulevard.

Callie shook her head at how different people can view the same person, place or thing so differently. Like Harlem itself, some people loved it. She, on the other hand loathed it. Every second was torture, but she couldn't leave until she avenged her man. She would only leave Harlem over their dead bodies.

"Ayo, check it," Peedi announced and pointed at the new face on the block. He liked what he saw but the boss got first dibs on all the new faces.

"Yoooo! That's son's chick. That nigga, Voodoo," Blu announced since he had been plotting on their block for a minute.

It was doing good numbers, so he made his move. Once he determined KT and Slime were the weakest links, he made his move on them. They quickly sold their man out to work for him. Blu would eventually have one kill the other, then kill that one and put his own people on the block.

"Want me to buss her?" a shorty asked since that's what he

did. Plus, he had just received a new gun but didn't get to shoot it yet.

"Nah, let me see what she talmbout," he said since he peeped how fine she was a while ago. If she was looking for the next dope boy dick to ride, she was in the right place.

"You Blu?" she asked even though he was dipped from head to toe in his signature color. The diamonds on his neck, wrist and fingers all had a blue hue, as well.

"Depends on who asking?" he replied and licked his lips. Peedi and the others took a few steps back so he could talk his shit except the shorty, who only took one step in case he had to buss something.

"My name is—shit you know who I am. I got some info for you!" she advised and waited for him to ask what it was. He didn't, so she continued. "I know them niggas KT and Slime slinging for you. They used to work with my man but kept pushing their own sacks on the side. Just like they doing now!"

"Okay, I see what's going on. You heard they the ones did yo' nigga, so you put me on them to get some get back!" he said and laughed. "I can dig it."

"So, you gonna do it?" Callie asked and the shorty listened for the nod to go buss something.

"Hell yeah!" he agreed and nodded. "After you let me hit."

"Hit what?" Callie asked genuinely. She was here on some murder shit, so that's all that was on her mind at the moment.

"This!" Blu announced and gripped her ass roughly. The slap was reflex like a doctor's rubber hammer to the knee. So was the one Blu unleashed after she slapped him. She hit the ground quicker than the slap that put her there.

"Bitch!" he shouted down as the shorty stepped forward.

"Want me to buss her?" he asked again.

"If she come on this block again, buss her ass!" he said to

34

him, while looking at her. He turned to Peedi with his next directive. "Keep an eye on that block. If a bag come off that street that ain't blue, kill them niggas!"

Callie picked herself off the concrete and slinked away. She had been ready to offer a few grand from the stash to kill the men, but all it cost was a slap. Her face stung from the blow but didn't stop her from smiling as a plan formulated in her head.

CHAPTER FIVE

allie was poor before meeting Voodoo, so she knew how to make the most of the hundred bucks she had left. She wouldn't touch the stash until she was leaving for good. Her first stop was to a discount store that carried cheap versions of everything. She knew where everything was since she had shopped there before.

A couple cheap bra and panty sets went into the cheap cart with wobbly wheels. The jeans ran small, but that was cool since her round ass made them look like a designer designed them. Socks and other items would carry her over until she could get to Atlanta, but first she had some plotting to do.

"Here we are," Callie said and laughed like a mad scientist as she entered a store Voodoo had taken her to several times.

She knew exactly where to go to find what she needed. Different drug factions around Harlem used different color packaging for the drugs. Blu sold his crack in blue bags, but Voodoo and the crew used to have green. After a moment of deliberations, she decided on yellow. She purchased a thousand bags, a box of baking soda and a few jars of baby food.

The block was bustling when she returned. She realized the world went on without Voodoo and eventually she would, too. First, revenge on those fools sitting on those steps slinging crack. Slime must have sensed her staring and looked up. They locked eyes until she disappeared into her building.

"Bitch want me, B!" Slime declared and gripped his dick.

"I want that work! That bitch holding out on us!" KT complained. Blu sold them a dream but was paying them less than they were making with Voodoo. Normally his word was pretty good. He just didn't respect these two. Now they definitely needed those nine ounces so they could sling on the side.

Meanwhile, Callie wasted no time once she got inside. She locked the new locks before digging out the coke. She ate the applesauce from the baby food jars before rinsing them out. By now, she could weigh by eye just as well as Voodoo did since she had helped him in this process so many times. She had no intention of becoming a dope girl but would help her man in whatever. Had Voodoo sold blow up balloons, her cheeks would have been sore from blowing them shits up.

"Don't go out bad..." she repeated like her dearly departed use to say as she pulled a surgical mask on her face. Voodoo told her a lot of dealers developed crack habits by inhalation of crack fumes while cooking up crack. She would not be one of them.

She filled a pot with water and put it on the fire. Next was water in the baby food jar which went inside the pot. She then stirred as she poured in the coke. Once she had a good boil, she added the baking soda while still stirring.

The magic happened and she soon had a nice cookie of pure glass. The junkies preferred her cooking to Voodoo's even if they didn't know it. It was certainly better than the mediocre rocks Blu was pushing.

The cooling period allowed Callie to shower the day away. Her brown skin prevented a bruise, but she could feel the welts from Blu's slap. Once again, she wished she was a killer so she could avenge herself. The vision of shooting KT and Slime made her smile. She saw herself walking back over to Blu's block and gunning him down as well. Of course, she would have to shoot his shooters and the bodies were piling up.

"Shit!" she fussed when she realized she couldn't kill anyone. She could set it up though, so she hurried the shower up and got to her plot.

Callie knew exactly what size to cut the dime sized rocks sold on the block. Some hoods sold twenties to maximize traffic while other blocks sold three-dollar hits or two for fives and had traffic like Grand Central Station at rush hour.

"Fuck that!" She decided and cut them even bigger. The bigger rocks barely fit inside the bags, but she managed. Now she had both quality and quantity, so she waited and watched from the window.

It wasn't long until KT slipped into his baby mama's building. With the extra money, he was making his decision to break her off. Slime took the opportunity to take a smoker up to a roof top to get topped off. She was already dressed down in a hoodie and jeans when she rushed down to the street.

"Free testers! Testers! KT and Slime got the testers! Spread the word! KT and Slime!" she said, while passing out free crack. The word of free crack spreads faster than brush fires, Delta variant and gossip all put together. Slime had just returned to his post when she wrapped up the first part of her mission. He was the next part, so she headed straight for him.

"Knew this bitch wanted me!" he assured himself as she

SA'ID SALAAM

neared. Instinctively, his hand gripped his dick once again because for some reason he thought chicks dig that.

"You need to drink some damn water!" The crack head griped and spit as she came out behind him. "Cum tastes like a bucket of salt!"

"Um, yeah," Callie said since that interrupted her train of thought on so many levels. "Oh! I found some of that work."

"Come on with it!" he urged and looked over at KT's baby mama's building. He was hoping to slime his partner too, but he had just stepped back out. Callie wanted him in on it since she wanted him dead too, so she waited.

"Sup?" KT wondered back and forth between the unlikely conspirators. Slime looked like he wanted to cry when she began to speak.

"I found that work, but y'all gotta break me off!" she declared and produced the cache of yellow bags. "Just gimme a band?"

"Ion know, yo. I..." Slime spoke up to talk her down on the price.

"Here!" KT quickly agreed and pulled a wad of cash. It was Blu's money, but this was a few thousand dollars' worth of work. There was no time to haggle, so he paid the price.

"You ain't find that bread he had put up?" Slime asked since she was finding shit.

"Nah, yo. His moms over in the Bronx was his bank. Y'all know you don't trust no hoes with y'all bread," she said and dipped back into her building before a flood of junkies returned for the yellow bags. They weren't the only ones to hear of the fat sacks of good crack.

"*How* ow the fuck err thing slow down all of a sudden?" Blu wanted to know when several blocks produced less than normal. "I know niggas still smoking crack, yo?"

"They still smoking," Peedi assured him. He would know since he just broke his mom off with her supply for the day. Some people might say it's fucked up to give your mother crack but fuck them folks, because it sure beats having your mother steal and suck dicks to support her habit. The woman was going to smoke, so he assured she could smoke with dignity.

"This the problem!" a worker said and produced a yellow bag filled with crack. "These supposed to be dimes, yo!"

"Who the fuck got them shits?" Blu wondered and looked around.

"Them niggas from the new block," he answered. He heard about them and went to cop one right out of KT's palm. "I even asked them for pacific blue sacks. He sold me this!"

"Specifically, dumb ass nigga. Damn, that bitch was telling the truth!" Blu sighed. He didn't regret slapping her but did regret not tapping that fat ass.

"Want me to buss 'em?" the shorty pleaded. He was ready to give the gun back since he was never allowed to buss nothing.

"Yes. Fuck yes!" Blu declared, getting inches from the young gun's face. "I want you to get this close to them, and knock they socks off!"

"Them niggas dead-dead!" Peedi laughed when the kid rushed off to complete his assignment. He wasn't the only one waiting for the action.

"This bitch stay watching me." Slime said and nodded as

he looked up at Callie looking down at him from her window. He was right too because the girl had posted up in the window for days, waiting, watching. She didn't even turn the TV on and ate her meals right there in the window.

"Or me," KT added since he had noticed her, as well. She had dated one dope boy, so maybe she was looking for another.

"About to give this bitch something to look at," Slime decided and whipped out the dick.

"Bruh." KT sighed and turned his head. "Just go up there."

"I just might," he said and blew a kiss at her. Callie just smiled but not at the kiss. She recognized the shorty from the other block when he turned on theirs.

"Here come Blu little mans. Get the blue bags out!" KT warned when he spotted the kid. They were prepared for this and quickly adjusted. Both were ready when he arrived. "Sup, fam?"

"This," the shorty replied and upped the burner to his face. He followed instructions and was so close, the barrel touched his cheek when he fired.

"Oh shit!" Slime exclaimed. He was right too, because KT's thoughts came out the back of his head and splattered on the bricks. He went for his gun, but the shorty already had his gun out.

"Un, un, un!" Callie sang along with the gunshots that made Slime dance as they tore into his torso. He went down, but the shorty stepped forward and pressed the gun against his nose and fired. "Yay!"

One thing about junkies is that they don't give a fuck! KT and Slime were still oozing blood and brain matter when the junkies started going through their pockets. They got the dope, cash and apartment keys to hit them too. The late comers had to settle for their sneakers and socks since everything else was gone. Callie stayed until the end of the show before moving. Now it was time to move on.

Her work here in Harlem was done. She finally dug the cash from the stash and headed out. Thanks to her neighbors, there was nothing to pack, so she headed down to the truck to make her escape. She had it cleaned but the coppery smell of blood still lingered on as she headed out of the city.

"I know ain't no drama like this down in Atlanta," she swooned and headed south. Lots of people move to Atlanta every year thinking they're escaping the drama of New York, Chicago and other places. Those people quickly find out just how wrong they are.

CHAPTER SIX

Atlanta, Georgia

Zenobia

"*H*and me the 'mote!" D-lo ordered when Zenobia breezed through the living room.

"Okay, first of all, what?" she snapped with the spunk and sass that either added to or took away from her yellowish good looks. Either accented or diminished the only incongruously white smile and slightly slanted eyes that belied her ethnicity.

Some people would guess there was a hint of Asian somewhere in her lineage. Actually, it was a trace of prenatal alcohol syndrome from a mother who liked to party all the time. It could have been worse, but the pretty young woman showed no other signs. Her quick temper and occasionally violent outburst were courtesy of growing up on the west side of Atlanta.

"The 'mote!" he stressed and pointed to the object just out of reach on the coffee table. Her head tilted curiously for a couple of reasons, prompting him to further explain. "The 'mote control!"

"Yeah, no that's a remote control," she said with a roll of her neck. It must have been a second of all in her mind because she came back with, "And third, that shit right there! All you gotta do is lean up!"

"A nigga high as fuck!" He laughed but did lean forward enough to get the remote. He was up, so he retrieved the half a blunt that put him in that state.

"So, I guess that means you not coming with me to see daddy?" Zenobia pouted. Not only would it be nice to have company on the ride, but they only had their daddy now that their mutual mother was gone. Both parents left the same night but only one would come back one day. Not this day, so she made the weekly drive to see him.

"Hell naw, cuz fuck him!" D-lo explained thoroughly.

"Whatever!" she fussed, spun and stomped out of the house. Her attitude got a wee bit worse when she looked at the twenty-year-old car she had to drive. It was behind the even older car her brother drove but his was souped up with all the bells and whistles drug money can buy.

"Don't you start yo' shit!" she warned the car before turning the ignition. It kept it's shit to itself today and crank right up. The CD player had been quit on her so turned the radio on for the ride.

An hour and a half later, she arrived at the medium security prison that housed her daddy. He was nine years into his twenty-year debt to society. Not quite to the down stroke but not the front end either. She had been coming alone since turning eighteen a year and a half ago.

Zenobia checked herself to make sure she was cute. She

liked looking nice for her dad but there were some cute guys in prison too. More than one had gotten in trouble for watching her instead of the wife or girlfriend in front of them. A couple of those wives and girlfriends were already in line and turned their noses up when she joined them.

I'on want nare one of y'all niggas, she thought to herself and turned her nose up, as well. That was settled so they all waited to get inside.

"Douglas Lowe," Zenobia announced as she presented her identification. The guard nodded along with her since she already knew who she was here to see.

"Step through the detector," the officer said.

Now it was her turn to nod since she knew the routine. That's why her heavy breasts were slung in a sports bra so there would be no underwire to ring the alarm. It only took one time to be pulled out of line and searched to learn that lesson.

Years later and she could still feel the feel of the manly woman's hands when patted her down looking for contraband. Zenobia huffed and sighed loudly even now. The detector stayed silent, so the officer said, "Have a nice visit."

"Thank you," Zenobia replied over her shoulder as she headed to the visitors' area. Her eyes scanned the mixed emotions etched faces from the good and bad news flowing to and fro. The cacophony of voices created a melodic din in the large open space. Then she saw him.

"Hey daddy!" Zenobia cheered when she spotted her father's smile across the room. The smile broadened and his arms spread as she neared.

"Hey there, Z!" Douglas said and wrapped his daughter into the safest place she had ever known. Zenobia hadn't felt safe since the day he left their home in handcuffs.

"You look good!" she cheered of his fresh cut and neatly

lined beard. Beyond that the forty-five-year-old looked like a twenty-eight-year-old with his daily workouts.

"You do too," he said and nodded approvingly at her outfit. The jeans were a bit tight for his liking, but that's what the kids wore nowadays.

"Thanks! Let me hit this machine before they buy them out!" she said and rushed over to the vending machines for burgers, snacks and sodas.

Douglas looked around at the men watching his daughter's backside there and back. The girl was the splitting image of his dead wife. He could only hope she didn't end up like her. Not dead, but not like her in life, that is.

"What?" Zenobia asked when she returned to his face twisted in thought. The smile spread instantly when he snapped out of the bad memory.

"Nothing, baby girl! Thank you!" he said and smiled at his favorite burger on the plate. They talked about school, life and the hood while he scarfed down the vending machine food. It fell right in the middle between world class gourmet and the garbage served in the chow hall.

"Slow down, daddy!" She laughed when he had to rush for a sip of soda to dislodge food from his esophagus.

"They got chicken guts and gravy tonight!" He laughed and took another huge bite. He had to be rescued by another gulp before he could talk again. "So, you got a lil boyfriend?"

"Uh, naw," she replied quickly but still had to pause to figure out what just happened with Carlos. A local dope boy her brother begged her to go out on a date with. He fed her and treated her wonderfully until she treated him to some pussy. Then never heard from him again.

"Mmhm," her daddy hummed but wouldn't pry. She was a good girl, getting good grades in school. Plus, they had a nice hustle going on that allowed him to still provide for her. They switched the subject a few more times until visitation drew to the end.

"I'm finna use the bathroom," she announced and cast a conspiratorial glance around the room. The guard was busy flirting with some man's wife as she slid past and into the bathroom.

"Just nasty!" She grimaced of the funk still hovering in the stall. She quickly peeled her jeans down and dropped her panties. A tug on the string removed the condom tucked inside. Luckily, she didn't have many miles on her vagina, so it stayed snugly in place.

She opened the knot and dumped the small balloons into her palm. Each was double wrapped since they contained enough drugs to kill her and a few more people a few times over. The red ones were filled with the weed her daddy liked to smoke. The blue ones were stuffed with the stuff that paid her two thousand dollars a week. The methamphetamine trade allowed her to go to school without flipping burgers or stripping.

The guard was still winking and smiling at the white woman while her white husband either didn't see or didn't mind. Zenobia traipsed by and slid back into her seat. She reached for the M&Ms on the plate but instead dropped the dope.

"My nigga!" her daddy cheered and began popping them into his mouth. He swallowed them whole and washed them down with the last of the soda before they stood.

"Okay, daddy. I'll see you next week," she purred as he pulled her into a comforting embrace.

"Hopefully this lawyer come through and you won't have to keep coming," he said and sighed. They only started hustling to pay the twenty-five-thousand-dollar lawyer fee. Felix Goldberg was supposed to be the best attorney in the city. He said he would get him home early, so Zenobia came up with the plan to come up with the money.

"He better!" she snarled. "For twenty-five grand, the bitch can answer the phone, or return a message!"

"Yeah," he said and sighed and gave her a final hug. As much as lawyers cost, they should respond to questions and phone calls. It had been a whole year since they paid but he had yet to get inside a courtroom. He watched her disappear through the door before being seated to await the strip search.

"Sup," the white man with the white wife nodded as he took a seat next to him.

"Same ole, same ole," Douglas said and turned away. Once his name was called, he stood and entered the shakedown room.

"Let them other guys calm down a bit," the officer said and laughed, since some men would still have hard ons from hugging and kissing wives and girlfriends at the end of the visit.

"Yeah," he agreed and stripped down to his boxer briefs. He watched as the officer went through his empty pockets and came up empty.

"Drop, bend and cough," the officer directed and inched forward for a closer look. He would never admit it to anyone, but this was his favorite part of the day. Not so much the looking up asses, but the obvious embarrassment the men had to feel. Except the men who liked men looking up their butt.

"Ugh!" Douglas coughed loudly and quickly stood to pull his drawers up.

"Had one earlier opened his mouth and when he bent over, I could see straight through him!" the cop joked but

Douglas just had a man look up his ass and wasn't in a joking mood.

"Cool," he said and accepted his clothes. He rushed to get dressed and hurried back to his dorm.

"Old school done struck!" a young gang banger acknowledged when Douglas hurried into his cell and put a flap on the window. He belonged to the gang called the Rollers and they usually robbed or extorted other prisoners.

"He from the city, tho," his fellow Roller advised. He knew it was a dangerous habit to shit where you eat. Atlanta is a small town as far as cities go. People did shit in prison that got them killed once they got home.

"Shit, I ain't!" the other Roller snapped. The gang may have originated in the city of Atlanta but was now statewide.

"Rallo said hands off the city!" he shot back. They went back and forth while Douglas leaned over the toilet and stuck the other end of his toothbrush down his throat.

It took a couple of gags before he began to toss his cookies, candy and dope. Saving them for last made the balloons the first things to come up. A quick count came up a few short so he stuck the toothbrush back down his throat. One more upchuck brought all the drugs up.

Douglas tucked the three red balloons aside and set out to deliver the blue ones. Each went for a thousand dollars and were paid for in advance except the first one since he was part of the plan.

"Steve," Douglas called and tapped on the cell door. It's a matter of respect to wait until invited into a man's cell, so he waited.

"Come on," the same white man with the same white wife cheered. He was down with the plan since the officer loved to flirt with his wife. The perfect distraction to swallow the dope. In exchange, he got a free pack of meth.

"Here you go, homie," he said and broke him off.

"Thanks. Still don't like that shit eater flirting with my Susie!" he grumbled but already had his works out. Doug nodded and turned to leave while he fixed up a fix to shoot into his arm. He made his rounds and earned his daily bread.

CHAPTER SEVEN

"*D*addy said hey," Zenobia lied when she returned from the visit and entered the smoke-filled home. The home their father bust his ass to build so they would always have a roof over their head. Her ungrateful brother didn't mind living, smoking and fucking here for free but still wouldn't speak to the man who provided it.

"Oh yeah! Tell him I said..." D-lo said and said nothing. It took his bright sister a second to catch his drift. She sucked her teeth, twisted her lips and stomped off to her bedroom.

"Girl, no!" she chided herself and shook her head to dislodge the thought of calling Carlos from her mind.

She liked him enough to go out with him out of all the guys in the hood. Mainly because her own brother kept suggesting it. She did and got smooth talked smooth out of her panties.

The very thought of getting tricked out some pussy made her sleepy, so she stretched out for a well needed nap. Naps are good most of the time, but sometimes that same bad dream was waiting on her like Freddy.

"I'll get it!" Zenobia sang as the doorbell chimed.

"Only thing you need to be getting is yo' narrow ass in yo' room!" her mother fussed. Zenobia knew by now a whooping came if she didn't move quick enough. Only when her daddy wasn't around though, because he would protect her.

Anitra Lowe looked at her daughter's backside as she rushed off. The twelve-year-old was starting to round out like her. She snarled at the thought of the child becoming competition. The doorbell chimed again, so she took a swig of gin from her water glass and straightened her dress.

"Hey," she greeted as she opened the door to let the man in.

"Shit, I thought he was here. You taking so long," Bobby said as he entered his friend's house. If David had been home, he could have just played it off like he was there to see him. He wasn't, so he stuck his tongue in her mouth and gripped her ass.

"Come on!" Anitra begged and dragged him into the bedroom she shared with her husband. Actually, he shared it with her since he paid for it and everything else in this house.

Young Zenobia heard a man's voice and listened even closer. Her face twisted when she heard them enter her daddy's bedroom and close the door. Fear prevented her from opening her door, so she pressed her ear against it and strained to hear.

Not that she could hear the slurps and slobs of the man's dick way down her mother's throat. This was partly her husband's fault for bragging about how good his wife's head game was. One reason married people should never reveal their bedroom business. The other reason is because that's just weird. Well, he kept bragging about that good head and Bobby decided to get him some.

"The whole dick, huh?" Bobby said as he completely disappeared down her throat. She gagged and nodded for a reply and kept right on delivering that killer head. It wasn't long until he delivered and skeeted down his friend's wife's throat. And that's pretty fucked up.

Zenobia may not have heard the blow job, but when they climbed on her daddy's bed and started humping, she definitely heard that. Like most twelve-year-olds in today's society, she knew what sex was. Knew more than a twelve-year-old probably should. Then again, she did hear that same bed squeaking and mama moaning from her mama and daddy her whole life.

"Ooooh!" Zenobia reeled and covered her mouth when she realized what was going on. The anger she felt then snatched her from her nap now.

"Man!" she moaned and popped up. The story got worse, and she was relieved to awake before reliving when bad went to worse. She realized what had pulled her from her slumber and got up to look.

"Niggas!" Zenobia grumbled when the bass rumbled through her window as a car pulled in the driveway. She peeped out the blind and saw Carlos in his Monte Carlo.

"So!" she whined and sat back down. Only for a second though and popped back up to get cute for him. She hit the bathroom while he rang the bell.

"Sup, my nigga?" Carlos asked as D-lo opened the door. He stepped in without being asked and D-lo didn't object.

"You here for my sister?" he asked and turned to call down the hall.

"Nah, nigga. I'm here about my bread?' he reminded him since he was late paying for the dope he was fronted.

"Oh! Okay, yeah! I'm almost done! Waiting on... and them, mmhm," D-lo stuttered and stammered.

"A'ight," Carlos warned him. With a reputation like his, you don't have to say much more than that. D-lo was in the streets and knew that rep was well earned.

"Tomorrow! On my mama!" he said and lied on his dead mother once again. Carlos already said what he said, so he turned to leave.

"Oh, hey," Zenobia practiced as she glossed her thick lips.

It was the perfect mix of aloof and 'boy where you been', so she rushed out to try it out. She slowed at the living room to make her appearance but only found her brother. "Where Carlos?"

"He gone. We had some business to handle," D-lo replied and lit another blunt of the weed he hadn't paid for.

"He ain't ask—I mean, he..." she whined.

"Bruh, I know you didn't?" He laughed. The disappointment on her face didn't faze him and he laughed anyway. Carlos was a known player but wasn't sure if Zenobia gave it up until her yellow face turned beet red. "Yeah, you did!"

"Fuck you, David!" she snapped and spun to go pout on her pillow.

"Wait!" he called after her. Zenobia stopped so her big brother could be her big brother. Carlos had used her, and he needed to whoop his ass for her honor. "Let me hold two bands?"

"Two rubber bands!" she fumed and stormed off.

"Bitch," he grumbled in general. Zenobia heard it and almost came back to tell him his mami was a bitch. She was her mami too, but a bitch, nonetheless. The dead woman was the reason they were living like this now.

D-lo shook his head and stood. He was going to have to hit the streets since no plan was knocking on the door.

"Let a nigga fuck your sister and the nigga still won't let you slide for a few funky ass thousand dollars!" D-lo had the audacity to gripe as he headed out to his car. He had sold some of the work he got on consignment but tricked the money off on Jordans and junkies. Most of the chicks he tricked with from the strip clubs were addicted to something —pills, weed, coke, meth or drama.

He still had a few pounds left, so he headed out to see if he could sell it for more than it was worth so he could pay

Carlos. It's never a good idea to get in business with dudes known to kill dudes about their business. D-lo wouldn't know a good idea if it walked right up to him and introduced itself.

"Finna go to the club and double up!" he cheered along with yet another bad idea. He would break the weed down into three quarters of a pound and sell them as pounds. Sure, it would create a new problem, but he would be able to pay Carlos back.

"D-lo!" the bouncer greeted. Everyone was happy to see him lately since he was a trick.

"Sup, AD," he said and sighed and dug into his pocket. He was already behind but had to give the man a tip. The only thing that parts sooner than a fool and his money is a trick and his money. A foolish trick like D-lo didn't stand a chance when the girls saw him.

"These hoes love me!" He allowed himself when a flock of birds rushed his table. They had a rule of first come, first served, so a particularly vicious bird made it first. She may have tripped one and shoved another but was still first.

"Hey, D-lo!" she sang and slid into the booth with him. Of course, she went straight for his crotch since nothing confuses a trick like a hard dick. She didn't play about her money, so she removed his dick to play with it.

"Sup, Platinum," he said and leaned back so she had room to stroke him. If he could get off here, it would save a few hundred bucks for a VIP room.

"You! What's in the bag?" she asked and spit on his dick for lubrication.

"Got pounds of gas. A band, I mean. Two bands each," he replied. The extra change would finance a trip to her tonsils.

Platinum stopped stroking for a moment while she thought. She used that same hand and pulled her phone from her boy shorts when a plan to kill two birds with one stone came to mind.

"Finna call my friend. He'll buy err thing you got. You gotta break me off, tho?" she asked but her friend came on the line before he could answer. Not that he would say no since he needed to sell it.

D-lo could only hear one side of the conversation, but it sounded good to him. Good enough to trick off and still have money left over to pay his debt, which was good since he would have tricked off anyway and dealt with the consequences.

"He on the way!" Platinum said and pulled him from the booth. "We got time to hit the VIP befo' he get here!"

"Bet that," D-lo said and followed behind that round behind jiggling in front of him. He paid a hundred of Carlos's dollars to the bouncer to get in the room, then another hundred to get into the dancer. Platinum tooted the booty up so he could hit while she checked her social media pages.

"You gotta finish up, playa!" she advised when her customer texted from the parking lot.

"Al... most... there..." D-lo said and switched gears. "Ughh! Shit! Whew!"

"Come on. Robbie outside!" she said and quickly stood.

D-lo snatched the rubber off and tossed it in the corner before pulling his pants back up. He had to rush to keep up and caught up before they hit the door. Platinum looked around the parking lot until a car flashed its lights to get her attention.

"Come on," she directed and led the way over.

"Hop in the back. Let my man up front," Robbie said when she pulled the door open.

"Sup, shawty," D-lo greeted as he hopped in next to him while Platinum sat behind him.

"What you got?" the buyer asked eagerly and looked at the bag.

"Few pounds of gas," he replied convincingly even though he was a few pounds short of the few pounds he was trying to sell. He held his breath, hoping the buyer didn't notice and prayed a little prayer he didn't have a scale.

"Looks good," Robbie said quickly and produced the cash even quicker. They made the exchange and D-lo was out of trouble, but only for a minute.

"Bet that. Here go my number," he said and sent his info. "I got tons of that shit. Holla when you ready."

"Definitely will. Soon!" he assured as D-lo stepped out. Platinum lingered two seconds behind.

"We straight?" she asked, sliding out of the back seat.

"Yup," he nodded and watched them head back inside. D-lo had just enough money to pay his debt but that whole 'trick and his money' thing bit him in his ass once again.

"Shit, I may as well go again?" he asked as if a hoe would say no. She didn't, so he spent another hundred at the door and one more on her tonsil. Then a hundred on the drinks that had him walking sideways when he left the club.

D-lo pulled out of the parking lot and headed to the intersection but never made it. Blue lights flashed as police cars pulled from every direction and boxed him in. He looked down at the bag he kept his drugs in and breathed a sigh of relief. He was still snatched from the car and unnecessarily wrestled to the ground.

CHAPTER EIGHT

"*B*ruh, why the fuck am I in here for?" D-lo demanded when someone finally entered the interrogation room an hour later. The icy cold air had sobered him completely up which was exactly what the cops wanted.

"I'll let my partner explain," the first cop said as the second cop entered behind him. No introduction was really needed but it was always fun. "You met Detective Robbie Gunter, I presume?"

"Yeah and you shorted me!" the buyer from the club said but he wasn't mad. It was still a felonious amount of weed.

"That trifling hoe!" D-lo growled and shook his head when he put two and two together. They added up to Platinum setting him up to get busted.

"Yeah, but you didn't know she was trifling before tonight?" Robbie asked incredibly. "Anyway, she owed me one or two."

He didn't go into detail about her selling him some pills when he was undercover in the club. She quickly gave up her connect in exchange for a free pass. The detective squeezed her for a few more dealers so he could work his way up the ladder. Dudes like this were bait to catch bigger fish. Real worms who would tell on the next man to avoid probation.

"So, you wanna go to jail or you wanna go home?" Robbie's partner asked. He loved Denzel in that role but very few ever wanted to go to jail.

"Your sister is downstairs already," Robbie added for good measure.

Zenobia had gotten wind of her big brother's arrest and made her way down to the precinct. He may have been the older sibling, but she took care of him instead of the other way around. All she found out was that he was up in narcotics and expected nothing less than ten thousand to bail him out.

"So, what I gotta do?" he asked as if he didn't know. Everyone knows if you don't have cash, it'll cost a little of your soul.

"Give up your connect," Robbie stated bluntly.

"Carlos?" D-lo asked, giving up his connect. The first cop looked at his watch and nodded.

"That's a new record," he said and nodded. Robbie smirked upon hearing the name. They had caught a few of his couriers before but none would give him up. The others figured breathing jail air was better than not breathing at all.

"Can you set up a buy?" Robbie asked.

"Hell naw," he quickly shot down. If he had paid attention, he would have seen this coming.

"Well, make a buy for us," the other offered. The marked bills would still make the case.

"Yeah!" D-lo answered, then pivoted. "No, I owe him money,"

"How much?" Robbie asked. It took some mental mathematics to come up with a figure that would leave some bread in his own pocket.

"Just give me ten racks. I'll pay him and buy some more," he decided. The cops agreed and set him free.

§♠.

"*J*ust wanna know why no one can tell me where my brother is!" Zenobia fussed. She didn't want to tie up her college money on bail but didn't want her brother in jail either. He was a high yellow, pretty boy and she heard what happens to high yellow pretty boys in jail.

Besides, she didn't want to stay alone in that house in the hood. A lame brother was better than no brother. Plus, she would ask their father to use the house for the bail and get her money back. She was about to really flip out until she saw her brother walking out the door.

"What the—" she wondered aloud.

"Hmph!" a woman waiting on word of a loved one grunted sarcastically. She had been here enough to know people who made bail used the other door. That was the snitch door he just came out of.

"Just a lil misunderstanding," he told his sister as he walked her out.

"Hmph!" the woman grunted at him again. D-lo shot her a bird behind his back as he led his sister away.

"What did you do? They say you got arrested!" Zenobia demanded and stopped. She crossed her arms indicating she wasn't budging until he told her something.

"Ain't nothing! A damn blunt!" he said looking around. "I was tipsy, so they made me wait. Take me to my car."

"I'll take you home! Figure the rest out on your own!" she fussed. Home was better than a jail cell, so he took the ride. He would get his car the next day and set up the buy with Carlos.

೩.

"*A*lways damn something with this nigga!" Zenobia grumbled when she finally got back into her bed. Dawn wasn't far off so her day was going to start off on a bad night. She hated sleeping while in a bad mood. It was an invitation for the bad dreams to come.

"I know!" Young Zenobia said when the doorbell began to chime. She did not need to get cursed out or threatened by her mother for her to go to her room.

Mrs. Lowe waited until the door closed behind her daughter before opening the door for her lover. He was here to fuck, so she led him straight to the bedroom she shared with her husband to fuck him. Zenobia had grown curious over the frequency of the visits and the noises coming from the room. So curious she snuck off to investigate. The hall floorboards were creaky, so she eased out her window and walked over to her parents' window. She had already set up a makeshift stepladder, so she stepped up for a peep.

The first peep sent her reeling and off the step. She wasn't sure if she saw what she saw so she stepped back up to see some more. Yup, she saw her daddy's friend with his face in between her mother's outstretched legs. Curiosity froze her in place to see what she didn't really want to see.

"I'm finna cum on yo' tongue!" Mrs. Lowe warned as her legs began to shiver.

"Mmhm," was all he could say with his tongue inside of her. Not that he could rightfully object, as many times he came on her tongue. He routinely nutted in the woman's mouth like she didn't have a husband coming home in a few hours.

Well, that was all pretty disturbing to the young girl, but it got worse. Mama kept her word and came on that man's tongue. He then crawled between her legs and shoved himself inside of her. He hoisted her white legs up on his black shoulders and absolutely beat it up.

Zenobia couldn't understand the splashing sounds and didn't know if her mother was in pain or pleasure. The grunts and fuck faces could have gone either way. Her mother went through those same convulsions once again when she came again.

Then she saw the first dick of her young life when the man rushed from her mother's private place to her mouth. Now it was his turn to grunt and groan as came on her tongue.

"Man!" Zenobia fussed and pulled herself from the dream and sleep. Just in time because the worst was yet to come.

§⋅

"*J*'m finna make some moves," D-lo said and hit the door. Zenobia didn't ask how but did peep out the window and saw that one of his girlfriends had came to pick him up.

"Good!" She sighed and sat back down. She was headed down to see their father tomorrow, so she would rest up for the rest of the day. Just no nap though because Freddy was waiting.

"You gonna give me some money for gas?" Juanita demanded before both of D-lo's cheeks touched the passenger seat.

"I told you I got you! Damn!" he snapped, and Juanita promptly stomped on the brakes.

"Hold up, nigga! You got me but you never get me!" she fussed since his word was no good at all. Sometimes having the pretty, light skinned boyfriend was more trouble than it was worth.

"I'ma get you today. I gotta pick up my whip from the impound, then go make a quick move and I'ma have some bread. We finna eat out, movie, whatever you want," he offered, and she accepted. Especially when he tossed in the, "Shoot, I might just get you pregnant."

"Okay! Ooh, my baby gonna have good hair!" she clapped and pulled off.

Juanita took him to the impound where a call from Detective Robbie waived the impound fees. Carlos headed straight over to the precinct to pick up the buy money. The police had ten thousand dollars of confiscated drug money waiting when he arrived. It included the couple thousand they took back from him last night. Minus what he gave to the bouncer and Platinum of course.

"Check," Carlos nodded and plotted. He owed two thousand and planned to spend five thousand. That would leave him three grand ahead of the game.

"Look, you're in a lot of trouble," Robbie lied. As far as trouble goes, this really wasn't too bad. Still, he used it to his advantage and mashed the gas. "Doing this is a good step towards getting out of that trouble."

"Ask him for coke. Or better yet, heroin!" the other cop added when D-lo picked up his phone to call Carlos. He nodded and made the call while they all listened in on the speaker.

"You got my bread, nigga!" Carlos barked as soon as he took the call.

"Hell yeah! Ready to cop something else. And I'm paying up front!" he said proudly.

"Hmph. I heard you got bagged last night?" he asked. A smart dealer wouldn't have to ask. He would have been done with dude. Then again, he wasn't that smart since he was talking drug business on the phone.

"DUI. My sister came and got me," D-lo quickly replied. There was a brief silence while Carlos processed the answer.

"A'ight. What you tryna cop?" he relented because cash rules everything around him.

"Shit, some boy. Some girl. Them hoes at the club be wanting it all!" he cheered.

"Fall through," Carlos said and clicked off before they could talk mone, which was exactly what D-lo wanted so he could keep the change.

"We got eyes on you the whole way," Robbie advised and handed over the cash. The two cops shared a 'would you look at this shit' glance at the way D-lo looked at the money. Obviously, cash ruled everything around him as well.

D-lo headed out to his car with the detectives close behind. They stayed close behind all the way over to Carlos's house in the hood. He had another house out in the burbs, but this was where all the action was.

"This dummy is going to blow it!" Robbie's partner fussed when the dummy looked back at them as he walked up to the door.

"His funeral," he said and laughed but only because he didn't give a fuck. He may have made his career by flipping snitches but had no respect for them.

"Sup, my nigga," Carlos greeted and looked up and down the block. He glanced over the detective's car but didn't take heed.

"First things first," D-lo announced and pulled out the buy money. He counted off his debt in one stack, while making a separate stack for the buy.

"A'ight," Carlos nodded at the count. He shorted him on both coke and heroin, but it was still more than enough.

"Check," he said as he accepted the drugs and turned to leave. He smiled towards Robbie and his partner as he got back into his car.

"Fucking idiot!" Robbie said, shaking his head. He used

his radio and called in the strike team who had discreetly assembled on the block.

D-lo didn't even make it off the block before they kicked Carlos's door off the hinges. They seized enough drugs, money and guns to send the man away for twenty years.

"So, we straight?" D-lo asked when he turned in the drugs back at the station.

"Almost. One or two more and your case goes away," Robbie said smugly.

"Oh, and we need it now or you're going in there with your boy. It won't be hard to figure out you set him up," the other cop added. This was pressure, and pressure can bust pipes.

CHAPTER NINE

"*What's wrong, baby girl?*" *David Lowe asked his daughter. They were close enough for him to tell something had been eating at the child for days. He was a father and that meant slaying any monsters under the bed or in the closet.*

"I'ma get in trouble..." Zenobia moaned and teared up. Her father knew then it had something to do with her mother.

Anitra was raised in an abusive home, so her parenting style was just that—abusive. David didn't know that until they already had kids. Now he had to check her on several occasions about how she treated their kids. To the point of threatening to whoop her ass if she beat his kids again. That didn't stop the verbal and mental abuse while he was at work. The lifestyle he wanted for his family meant he was almost always at work.

"No you ain't. Just tell me," he said and she broke down in tears just trying to get it out. The neighbors picked up on the treason, so the kids started to tease her about what her white mother was doing.

"Bob-Bobby be coming over here when you go to work," was as far as she could get before breaking down once more. It was more than

enough since there's only one reason a man would be coming over while he was at work.

"It's okay, baby," he assured her and stroked her curls. "See, you not in trouble!"

"You gonna tell him not to come here no more!" she demanded hotly. The daddy's girl didn't take kindly to anyone making a fool out of her daddy. She saw the man with his dick in her mother's mouth, then she turned around and kissed her daddy with that same mouth.

"I sure am," he agreed and kissed her goodnight.

David was busy, not dumb. He had a sneaking suspicion something was amiss but was too busy working to pay for all this shit. It would explain why he wasn't getting the full treatment in the bedroom anymore. She was saving it for someone else. His so-called friend at that.

"What's wrong with you?" Anitra asked when David entered the bedroom.

"Huh?" he asked since he couldn't see how screwed up his face was until he saw it in the mirror. He tried to fix it with a smile.

"Okay." She laughed at the phony smile and slid in beside him. Her husband reached over between her legs but was stopped before he got where he was trying to go. Something she had been doing more of lately. He could almost gauge how long this was going on since she started saving it for Bobby.

"What's wrong?" he asked, knowing what was coming. She had been keeping him distracted another way so he wouldn't catch on.

"Think I got a UTI," she replied quickly as she dipped under the covers. The blow jobs put him right to sleep and he didn't even notice.

"Hmph," he huffed but now wasn't the time to complain. Instead, he plotted and planned until he exploded on her tonsils. She gulped it down and cuddled up next to him. David was good and relaxed from the blow job. He decided to think good thoughts about his daughter's news. Surely his wife wasn't creeping with his friend in his house. Either way, he was about to find out.

The next morning started like most. David Jr. and Zenobia were out of school for the summer and usually slept in. Anitra fixed his breakfast and loaded his lunch box like every other day. Only difference was this time he slipped into his children's rooms to say goodbye.

"Here. Take your sister to the show," he told his namesake son before he started going by D-lo.

"With me?" he asked and accepted the money.

"I just said...yes, with you," he said without getting upset. "Always look out for your sister!"

"Oh," David said without the 'kay', since he was suspect, even at that age. Zenobia was sleeping so soundly when he went into her room, so her daddy let her sleep. She stayed up late watching TV, so he settled for a kiss on her forehead.

"Everything okay?" Anitra asked since her husband seemed slightly off kilter.

"Guess we'll see," he said ominously. She could have taken the warning, but some people do foul shit because they're just foul. It gives them a thrill to lie, cheat and steal. Anitra was some people.

Well David drove to work and clocked in but didn't do much work. His mind was elsewhere while he watched the clock. His son was like some people, just like his mama, so he took the money and snuck out without his sister. He was a trick already, so he went to get candy so one of these fast ass girls would let him hunch.

Around eleven, he sighed and clocked out. He always kept his pistol in the trunk once he had kids in the house. He moved it from under the spare tire to his lap and drove home. It wasn't so much Bobby coming over that had him seeing red. It was whatever his daughter saw that had her so disturbed.

"Well..." David Sr. signed when he saw Bobby's car up the block. Not directly in front of the house but he lived across town, so it may as well have been parked in the living room. He parked down the block and walked home.

"Uh-oh," a neighbor said when he saw not just the man, but the

look on his face. He had peeped the creeping a while back, but it wasn't his business. Still, he liked the man and did what he could. "Hey, David. How the kids?"

"Mmm," he grunted and missed the hint. The man tried to remind him of what was more important, but he was in his zone. He could only shake his head as the man marched on.

David deliberately left the back door open to avoid that creaky spot in the hall. Not that it would have been heard over the sexual symphony coming from his bedroom. Her moans and curses blended in with his grunts and growls on top of the bedsprings singing backup.

"I'm finna come all over this dick!" she vowed and did that. The pace picked up when Bobby really threw the dick into overdrive.

Ironically, it was the thought of his darling daughter having to hear this is what really pissed David off. The tears in her eyes when she tried to tell him about this just made him kick the door that much harder. His head tilted curiously when he saw the position his friend had his wife twisted in. She laid on her side with Bobby straddling one leg with the other straight up towards the ceiling.

"Uh-oh!" Bobby said when he looked over and saw his friend with the gun. Only his stroke had got so good to him, his hips kept on thrusting.

"It's not what it looks like!" Anitra shouted when she looked up. It was that insult to the injury that got her shot. The gun seemed to lift by itself and fire a round right into her lying mouth.

"You ain't have to do that! Bruh, you shot my bitch!" Bobby snapped. He had the audacity to be mad enough to come after David in his own bedroom except David had a gun.

"Go with yo' bitch then," he said and shot him in the stomach. He walked right up and lifted the gun to his forehead and.

"No!" Zenobia shouted from behind him. David froze as his daughter looked around the gory scene. She processed her dead mother and screamed once again.

"No!" Zenobia screamed loud enough in the dream to

wake herself up. She found herself in her bed soaked with sweat. "Fuck!"

Zenobia looked at the clock and realized it was time to get on the road. First, she had to shower and get the package ready. School was right around the corner, and she needed to get ready. After showering the sweat from the bad dream away she loaded the balloons and slid them inside of her. There were other ways to make a living, but this was by far the easiest.

"The hell wrong with you?" she snapped at her brother with the long face on the sofa.

"Who?" D-lo asked but she just put a hand on her hip since no one else was in the house. He looked so sad, she actually felt sorry for him.

"You good, bro?" she asked again but softer and rubbed his curls.

"Naw," he admitted.

"Well, just chill. I'll help with whatever it is when I get back from seeing daddy," she said and headed for the door.

"Z!" he called and stopped her before she got outside. Something changed his mind, so he let it and her go. "Never mind."

"Just weird," Zenobia said to herself as she headed to her car. The world seemed off but those nightmares always knocked the wind out of her.

She turned on the radio and listened to the mindless music to take her mind off of her task. Mainly millionaire rappers rapping about killing each other. Smuggling drugs into a prison was a serious matter, so she took it seriously. Coming every week made the guards relax since she was a regular. Most admired the girl for riding with her daddy even after he killed her mother. She was a daddy's girl for life, even after the death of her mother.

Zenobia initially dealt with the guilt by smoking weed and messing with boys. It wasn't until her father convinced her that he already knew. He didn't but she believed it and gave up both bad habits and buckled down in school. She had yet to declare a major but breezed through her freshman year.

Her senses tingled when she pulled into the prison parking lot. Nothing looked out of the norm, so she continued like she normally would. She filed in the back of the line and made small talk with the other regulars. She didn't even notice the not so regulars who got in line behind them.

This bitch, Zenobia moaned mentally when she saw the same stud officer who felt her up years ago. She was looking so intently at her, it made her uncomfortable. All she could do was ignore her so she could see her daddy.

"Excuse me. Zenobia Lowe?" a lieutenant asked even though he picked up her ID card when she began to sign in. She fought back the sarcasm and it's a good thing since she was quickly surrounded. The plainclothes officers who got in line behind her moved forward to block her escape.

"Yes? Is my daddy okay?" she wondered and struck a nerve with the stone-faced stud. Here she was in a world of trouble but she's worrying about her daddy. She was on some bullshit in her own right but still recognized real.

"Your father is fine. We got a report that you are attempting to introduce contraband into the facility," he explained.

"Huh?" Zenobia asked, looking around for an escape. Finding none she scanned for a friendly face but didn't see one of those either. She was smart enough to play dumb when she needed to. "I'on even know nobody named no contra-band! So, I'm supposed to introduce him?"

"Officer McMillan is going to search you," the lieutenant said and nodded at the stud.

"Awe, man!" Zenobia grumbled and placed her hands on the wall to be patted down.

"No, searched. Entering the premises gives us the authority to strip search you," he explained.

"This way," the stud directed and took her by the arm. Zenobia felt her power and knew she couldn't have pulled away if she tried. She just shook her head and accepted her fate as they entered the bathroom. "Look, if you got something, give it up now and I got you."

"Got me?" she asked for clarity. Got you isn't always a good thing. People get got every day and it's rarely a good thing.

"Make it disappear, but..." she said and licked her thick lips with the purple tint from smoking menthols.

"But what?" Zenobia shot back indignantly.

"If you want to go to jail, cool with me. If you wanna go home, let me lick that pussy," she explained in detail and extended her palm. "Either way, you coming off that pack. Now what you tryna do?"

"Man..." she said and pouted since her choices were fucked up either way. She unzipped her pants and pulled them down to her thighs. The stud licked her lips once again when the panties came down. Zenobia pulled the string and handed over the drugs.

"Turn around and bend over," the stud said hoarsely from desire. Zenobia seemed confused as she complied. There wasn't enough time or space to get it like she wanted to, so this would do. She leaned in and inhaled deeply. "Damn that thang pretty!"

"Oh!" she reeled when the first tongue touched her box in her young life. There was no pleasure when the stud sucked and licked her vagina and anus. In fact, a tear got loose at her consenting to be molested.

She couldn't enjoy it, but the stud was grunting and moaning like she was having a ball. She was but she had done this before and knew she had to wrap it up. She burrowed her tongue up in her box one good time and stood.

"Can I get dressed now?" Zenobia pleaded as McMillan stuffed the drugs into her own pants.

"Yeah," she said and watched the girl dress like guys watched girls dress. She led the way back out where several agencies waited for word.

"Well?" the lieutenant asked eagerly. Everyone, including Zenobia turned to her for the answer.

"Clean as a whistle," the stud said, lifting her palms and shrugging.

"Shit!" one of the plainclothes cops fussed.

"You're free to go, ma'am," Zenobia was told. She turned and rushed back out of the building and to her car. The close call and molestation made her just want to crawl back in bed and hide under her Dora the Explorer comforter. The stud's voice behind her nearly caused her to take off running.

"What now?" she pleaded as the manly woman caught up with her.

"I'll talk to yo' daddy. He good people," she said since she understood the close call had her frazzled. "Look, game up tho. Don't brang no more dope down here. Oh and, your brother is a real piece of shit!"

CHAPTER TEN

"$\mathcal{J}$ know your bitch ass see me calling you!" Zenobia screamed into her phone when her brother's phone went to voicemail again.

She had been calling the whole way home but didn't leave the message until she arrived at the house and didn't see his car. She turned quickly when a car barreled up into the driveway behind her and skidded to a stop just short of hitting her car.

"Carlos?" she actually had to ask since his handsome face was twisted unrecognizable from anger.

"Where your bitch ass brother!" he demanded as he walked up on her with his teeth clenched and fist balled up.

"I'on know where that fuck boy at! He just put the folks on me!" she snapped just as harsh and got back in his face.

"Yo, tell that nigga it's up!" he said and stomped back to his car. Zenobia took a second to admire how fine he was, even when mad. She quickly shook it off since she was mad at him too.

"This nigga been inside me and ain't even say hey. How you doing!" she grumbled her way back inside the house.

She stomped into his room but he wasn't there either. Even after checking under his bed. Everything he owned was still in his closet which meant he was coming back eventually. Her phone rang in her hand, and she saw it was her father calling again. He had called several times on the drive back home but this time she took the call.

"Hey, daddy." She sighed when the prerecorded messages finished warning that the call was being recorded.

"You okay?" he asked since he heard from Officer McMillan what happened.

"Yeah. Your damn son," she reported. Ironically, this was her first time reporting anything on him while he used to tell everything she did. He had been a snitch since they were kids. The line went silent for a moment while that sank in.

"Wow! Why? I mean, wow!" David Sr. said and shook his head. "He's always been like his mama."

Now it was Zenobia's turn to be silent. It took her coming of age to realize her mother got what she had coming for the extreme disrespect. It wasn't the fucking of his friend that got her killed. It was fucking him in her father's bed that did that.

"He told on some other folks. They looking for him," she said.

"Keep him away from the house! That's my house! I don't want him nowhere near it or you!" he shouted. Zenobia flinched since it was the first time her daddy yelled at her. She knew it was for her own good just like everything he had ever done.

"Okay, daddy," she agreed, nodding like she had done when she wore pigtails. "I'ma come back down next week?"

"Yeah, but no," David said and shook his head too. "That's dead. I'll find another way."

"But—" she began to protest since she needed the money too.

"But nothing! That's dead. You finna go back to school. I got you, baby girl!" he insisted and shut down her protest.

"Okay, daddy." She sighed and basked in the bliss of having a daddy. Even if separated by miles and years until they could be together again. The conversation took a turn for the better as she filled him in about college.

§▲

"*T*he fuck?" D-lo wondered when his key didn't work. He double checked the key, then the house number before trying again.

Zenobia had to YouTube how to change the lock since she intended to honor her father's instruction to keep her brother out. Except she didn't think about the back and side doors. He staggered around to the back of the house and used the same door his daddy used to ambush his mama.

"Shit!" Zenobia fussed when noises woke her up. She grabbed the only weapon she had and rushed towards the danger. Sometimes she had more heart than smart. "Fuck you finna do with that? You couldn't even hit a softball when you used to play!" D-lo laughed as she lowered the bat.

"You can't be here!" she demanded and blocked his way.

"Why not? This is my house. I live here!" he demanded back and pushed past her. His speech was slurred and vision blurred from being pissy drunk.

"Uh, this is daddy's house and he said he don't want you here!" she relayed on his behalf before going in on her own. "And cuz you put the folks on me! Don't try to lie. Detective Robbie told me!"

"Oh," he relented when he heard the name. "Shit you young, and a girl. They wasn't finna do nothing."

"You not staying he—" she was saying when a flash of light from a car pulling into the driveway stole their attention.

"Go to your room!" D-lo insisted and pulled a pistol from his waistband. Zenobia wanted to protest but the sight of the gun and the look in his eyes killed all arguments. She has seen that look before in their daddy's eyes when he killed their mama.

"Come on out here, fuck boy!" Carlos shouted from outside and fired a shot through the window. He gave a nod to his partner who slammed one of the mazaltoff cocktails against his car. Carlos fired a shot at it and ignited it.

"My car!" D-lo shouted back and fired back through the same window. Another nod sent another cocktail sailing. This one hit the front door and started a fire.

D-lo watched as the sidekick lifted the last firebomb and fired at him. The slug slammed into his chest causing him to drop the bomb at his own feet. His screams rang out louder than the back and forth gunfire. Carlos flipped the switch on his Draco and let it rip through the burning house.

Run! rang through Zenobia's mind as smoke seeped into her room. She stood just as a flurry of the 7.62 rounds tore through her wall. The rounds barely missed as she shimmied out the back window into the back yard. Meanwhile, her brother rushed out the front door to confront the threat to his family.

"Argh!" D-lo shouted as he rushed out with his gun blazing.

"Yeah, nigga!" Carlos screamed and took aim. Both ignored the sting and burn of bullets entering them while trying to kill their enemy. Both would succeed.

D-lo took a flying leap off the porch but slugs from the

chopper suspended him in the air. The bullets knocked chunks out his back while he was in the air. He would be dead by the time he landed. One last tug on the trigger made sure he had company on his trip to hell. A lone bullet tapped on Carlos's forehead but it didn't wait for permission to enter.

Carlos sat down Indian style and died while D-lo dropped dead from the air. Zenobia had hopped a few fences and was on the next block when the gunfire finally stopped. Still, she didn't dare go back as the fire lit the night air with a yellow glow.

Sirens filled the air as cops and firetrucks as she huddled behind a car. It was only after a crowd of spectators gathered that she ventured over to her house. Zenobia joined the band of spectators who speculated about the burning home with the dead men out front.

"I hope my girl Z ain't in there!" one of her old classmates from school moaned. They weren't particularly close in life but she was going to claim her in death.

"Awe, man!" Zenobia moaned when the fire spread from D-lo's car to hers. It combined with the burning house meant she had officially lost everything she had.

CHAPTER ELEVEN

Brentwood, California

Penelope

"*A*ll these niggas be sweating me, tryna be sexing me. Pussy ain't free, gotta pay to see, cheap ass niggas ain't the way to be..." P-money rapped along with her favorite female rapper. The pounding music made her twerk and sling her long dreadlocks. A steady knock on the door disturbed her groove so she turned the music off.

This was one of the most prestigious universities in southern California after all. No one really wanted to hear about Lady Crack talking about renting her vagina for cash and drugs. Or her latest platinum offering about eating dick for breakfast. The other students were more interested in bachelor's, masters and doctorates.

The loud music wasn't her coed comrades' only complaint about the ratchet chick. P-money kept a steady flow to and from the dorm and her room. Guys, gals, athletes, nerds and everyone in between. A few professors heard about her as well but met her off campus.

"A'ight! Damn!" she fussed when the door kept knocking.

"What you got, Penny?" a nerdy white student asked eagerly when she pulled open her dorm door.

"That's P-money, yo!" she reminded and pulled a bag of pills. "Just oxy today, Oliver."

"Beggars um, you know, um..." he said and tried to recall the saying, but the tiny shorts and wife beater had him thoroughly confused. He would probably cure cancer one day but zero chances at ever touching the perky breast. He looked up into her green eyes, but they were just as alluring so he went back down to her breast.

"Yeah, no you can't afford them," she teased and laughed.

"No, I'm not rich or popular like Ice," he shot back since he didn't like getting laughed at. No more than P-money liked to get lied on.

"What's that supposed to mean?" she dared. There had been a lot of chatter and whispers following a recent date with the all-star point guard named Ice.

"Oh, everyone knows! The whole basketball team!" he exclaimed almost as loud as the slap that followed. The nerd looked shocked by the slap that left a red handprint on his white skin. His eyes welled with tears before he tore off screaming, "Mom!"

"The fuck they talmbout," P-money said, while pulling up Ice's IG account. A smile began to spread when she saw he posted a picture of the two of them on a recent date. The caption below wiped that smile away just like when she slapped the nerd.

Shout out to P-money for taking one for the team #whitegirlhead #sheswollowed. #superfreak #teammascot

"Lying Mother fucker!" she growled and turned for the

door. She grabbed the aluminum bat from behind the door on the way. It probably would have been better to pull some sweats over the booty shorts and wife beater but there was no time. Her honor had been attacked and that had to be addressed. Something people who lack honor would never understand.

"Uh-oh!" someone said when P-money stomped through with the bat in hand. The angry white girl with the bat had a trail of people following her as she crossed through the parking lot.

The athletes had their own dorm in an attempt to keep down the sexual attacks. It didn't help since the basketball, football and baseball players just brought their dates and victims there. There where Ice brought P-money to smoke after they ate. Something happened inside the room but not what he was reporting on his social media feed. Facebook, Twitter, and Instagram have replaced NBC, CNC and HLN as the source of news nowadays. He reported it and they believed it.

P-money intended to march into the dorm and kick his door until he opened it. Then bash his forehead in with the bat. However, his 2021 Acura NSX parked out front gave her a better idea. All phones were pointed at her when she jumped on the roof of the car and took a swing. Ice was in his room when she launched her attack on his vehicle.

"Ride that dick! Ride it bitch!" Ice demanded the girl riding his dick backwards. He only called her a bitch since he didn't catch her name when he brought her home last night. Ironically, the dick was the only ride she had coming this morning. He was going to put her out right after she put out. He gave the fat booty a slap and demanded, "Ride, that, dick!"

"Yo, Ice! Look out your window!" a teammate shouted and

banged on the door. His alarm went off at the exact same moment and he tossed the chick aside and rushed over to the window.

"The fuck! Get off my car bitch!" he shouted as P-money shattered the driver's window.

"Bitch, huh?" she shouted back and bust out the passenger window.

There weren't many windows left, so he ran out his door and out into the parking lot to save his one hundred and fifty-seven thousand dollar car. That was so pressing, he forgot his drawers, pants and shoes. All phones turned to the six-foot, seven-inch point guard with the seven- inch dick bobbing in the fresh air.

"Get the fuck off my car!" he whined and reached to pull her off. A crack of the bat knocked his hand away and broke a finger.

"Tell the, truth!" she shouted with each swing of the bat. Each swing cost several thousand dollars as it dinged and dented.

"About what! You know you're a freak!" he insisted and lost both mirrors. "Okay! Okay! Just chill!"

"You chill!" she snapped and broke out the back window.

"Go, P-money!" someone shouted and turned on his car system. She responded by twerking as she knocked the wing off the back.

"I fucked the team?" P-money growled.

"No! It was a joke!" Ice pleaded but she kept swinging.

"Did I fuck you?" she asked in between damages.

"No! You wouldn't give it up!" he admitted. His spurned ego prompted him to lie on his dick and destroy her reputation.

"Tell them what happened!" she demanded with all cameras rolling, ready to capture the confession.

"I ate you and jacked my dick!" Ice hurried in hopes of saving the rest of his vehicle.

"Ate what?" she dared and lifted the bat.

"Your ass. I ate your ass and jacked my own dick! She wouldn't let me fuck!" he admitted. "There! You fucking happy?"

"Ecstatic!" P-money cheered and hopped down. She had turned down a lot of dick in exchange for keeping her virginity. And damn sure wasn't going to lose it to a lie on IG.

"Go, P-money! Go, P-money!" the crowd cheered. Except campus police had just pulled up so the only place P-money was going was jail.

$\&$

*W*hite has its privileges, but wealth has more. That's why Penelope Manning AKA Penny AKA P-money of the Palm Beach Mannings wasn't worried about a thing. She was rapping and twerking in the holding area until her parents arrived by helicopter.

"Excuse me, Miss Manning. Your parents are here," a polite officer advised when she saw him watching her work her twerk.

"Mmhm," she huffed and followed him out to where her parents were. Her biological mom was deceased, and she still hadn't quite accepted the step mom only a few years her senior.

"Oh, Penelope," the newest Mrs. Manning said, shaking her head at what she was wearing. Her father looked down at the ground since yet another embarrassing episode weighed down his head.

"Hello father, Misty," she said and lifted her chin proudly.

She stood up for her honor and was ready to accept whatever came along with it. Or so she thought.

"The Dean is waiting," the chief of campus police reminded.

"And he can wait! We just donated a library to this place!" Mrs. Manning fussed. Mainly because she could have bought a lot of shit for herself with that kind of money. She was selfish and didn't get the whole philanthropy thing.

"Tell him we're on our way," Mr. Manning said and led the way. Just over to the administration building since his wife led every other way. She brought nothing into the marriage and home except a youthful vagina and augmented breast. It wasn't long until she was running the household. Except when it came to his daughter that is.

"Hello, Mr. Manning!" the Dean's secretary cheered when they arrived. She hit the intercom to announce their arrival.

"Send them in," he replied and stood.

"I'll head back to the dorm. See you later," Penelope said as Penny now.

"Okay, dear—" her father began until his wife pinched him. "No, you will stay here!"

"You hired this band, so face the music!" Misty said as they entered the office.

"I'on know what kinda trailer park euphemism that is," Penny snickered to the secretary. They shared a quick laugh on the way inside.

"Always a pleasure, Robert!" Dean Hamilton lied as he stretched his hand out to his old friend. They had actually attended this same school together a hundred years or so ago. One went on to run the joint while the other ran an international shipping conglomerate.

"You lie like a toupee Bill!" He laughed and shook that

hand. They both let out a sigh that meant they would rather be downing martinis somewhere than dealing with this.

"Have a seat, please," the Dean offered and went back around his desk to take his own seat. The Mannings sat front and center while Penny opted for the tufted leather sofa. "Well, we had a... well... another incident regarding Penelope."

"How much is this one going to cost?" Misty wanted to know. "Pay the man so we can get out of here."

"College makes you queasy I bet," Penny quipped. She felt some kind of way that her mom had a few degrees to help her father grow their business. Then a floozie with fake breasts moves right in the house.

"I'm afraid this one can't be fixed that simply. The school's star point guard suffered a broken finger. We were the odds on favorite to win the NCAA tournament this year," he said and sighed since that cost the university tens of millions of dollars.

What he didn't mention were the reports rolling in about that same point guard's sexual assault reports. Penny standing up gave the women and teens the courage to do the same. Sometimes you need to take a baseball bat and beat the truth out in life.

"I'm sure, there is something we can work out," Mr Manning offered like a blank check.

"If not for the video." Hamilton sighed and hit the remote. "It's viral."

"Oh my!" the father said while the step mom shook her head. Only Penny was amused at her alter ego twerking up on the hood of the car while swinging a bat like Harley Quinn.

"Heeey!" Penny sang since someone added music to the many videos captured and posted.

"I see," Mr. Manning said even though he wasn't looking.

He knew this was bad, just not sure how bad. Until his friend spoke up and told him.

"It's over my head and out of my hands," he said and sighed apologetically. The father knew what that meant since he had attended college. The stepmom hadn't and had a question. "There are allegations of drug sales, as well. Too much to sweep under the rug."

"What does that mean?" Misty asked, looking back and forth between the older men. Penny picked her head up and zoomed in as well.

"I'm afraid every camel has that straw that um, well," the Dean stammered. He cleared his throat and continued, "Penelope Manning does not meet the standards of this university. As such, she has been expelled. Effective immediately, she must move from the dorm and leave campus."

CHAPTER TWELVE

"Welp." Penny sighed as she finished packing.

"Yeah," her dad agreed. He stayed behind to help while Misty flew back home in the helicopter. He paid for the Benz his daughter drove, so it was only right he helped fill it with her belongings and drive it back. Several customers had stopped by to cop while she packed but she ran them off.

"It'll be okay dad," she said but left out how it would be. Only because she had no idea.

"I'm sure!" He agreed but had one request. "Any way you can put on a little more clothes? A lot more actually."

"Sorry, dad." She laughed at his red cheeks and grabbed a pair of sweats. She dipped into her bathroom one last time and came out covered in cloth. Her head dropped when it was time to walk out the door for the last time but her father wouldn't hear of it.

"Absolutely not! You're a Manning! You lift that head and walk with dignity!" he demanded. He wasn't born with a silver spoon in his mouth but bust his ass to make sure she was. He would have loved some sons, but God didn't decree him any.

"Sorry, dad," she said, meaning all of it. This, the last, and most likely the next fuck up. Her father didn't get to reply because a crowd of people had gathered when news spread of her leaving. The silent mob just watched until someone broke the ice.

"Long live P-money!" a man screamed and set off a parade of well wishes.

Mr. Manning looked down at his daughter and knew she was going to be alright. The mistakes she made came from being a privileged white girl. Mistakes he didn't get to make since he started from zero. He took the keys and opened the passenger door for his celebrity daughter.

"P-money out dis bitch my niggas!" she declared and got a thunderous send off. The cheers were heard all the way off campus.

"We don't use the n-word, dear. It's derisive, mean and disgusting!" he said firmly. Firmer than most things since it was dear to his heart.

"I said nigga, not nigger. There's a difference, daddy!" She laughed at his ignorance for not knowing the difference. Either one can get your ass kicked around the wrong people.

"I don't like it either way! Too much hate associated with it. I don't want to hear it again?" he said but with the inflection of a question and turned for an answer.

"Yes father," she said but didn't agree. There were still too many other things that had to be addressed to hover on "a" versus "er".

"Remember when you were five and wanted to be a cowgirl?" Mr. Manning sighed and smiled at the fond memory.

"Yeah and you and mom bought me cowboy boots, hats and a horse!" She laughed.

"Then you wanted to play piano, so we bought a grand piano and hired the best teacher in the state," he recalled.

"Yeah, then I changed my mind and wanted to play the drums. Then softball," she admitted.

"Don't forget when you *'identified'* as a boy a whole summer and we had to buy you all those boy clothes," he reminded her.

"Guess I've always been a screw up, huh?" she wondered aloud.

He didn't know about her deciding she was actually a lesbian in high school since people kept calling her one since she wouldn't put out. Her lack of premarital sex had to mean she was gay. God forbid a person have morals and respect for themselves. That didn't last very long when she found out lesbians had to eat pussy. She wasn't with that part and quit that just like all the other whims in her life.

"Yup!" he nodded emphatically. She wanted to drop her head again but once again he would not let her. "But I've always had your back. I always will!"

"Can you dump Misty then?" Penny laughed even though she was so serious.

"Wish I could sometimes..." He sighed. A few minutes of good sex wasn't worth the hours, days and years of dealing with the woman. He figured her coming from nothing would make her appreciate something. Except it backfired and made her want everything. "Never mind me, though. You still need to finish school!"

"Yeah, I know," she agreed and nodded. He knew her father expected her to run the company one day. The stockholders would have a lot to say about a college dropout running the billion-dollar business. "See now, if you had let me attend Atlanta college none of this would have happened!"

"Okay, let me get this straight..." Mr. Manning began but had to pause to laugh. "Had I let my sheltered, privileged, spoiled, white teen daughter attends a HBCU all the way across the country, she would have gotten in less trouble than in the best university in California."

"Knew you would understand," she said and laughed even though it sounded preposterous out loud. The two enjoyed the conversation and each other on the ride to the mansion. It would come to an end once they arrived since Misty was there.

&

"*H*mph," Misty huffed when she saw her husband and stepdaughter pulling around the circular drive on the monitor. She may have been the newest addition to the house but enjoyed it better when she had it all to herself. Especially the pool where she could lay out naked and get a full body tan.

The pool man missed a bunch of spots since he was too busy checking her out. He had a handful of dick in his hand just tugging and stroking until she rushed to cover up since her husband was home and went inside to meet them.

"Too slow today!" she teased since he didn't get to finish. Then went to hug her husband as if she hadn't just given a free show to the pool guy. "Hello, dear husband. Welcome um, Penelope."

"Home. As in house my mom helped build," Penny reminded her since the interloper seemed to forget after redecorating all traces of the original Mrs. Manning away. Penny turned to head to what used to be her room but was stopped.

"Eh-em," Misty cleared her throat towards her husband.

"Yes, um we made some changes," he reluctantly admitted. "Misty made your old room her Pilate studio. You can use the guest room. It's been redone!"

"Like for guests?" Penny said but only because she wanted her dad to hear how it sounded. He lowered his head and ducked off to the safety of his study. Misty hated the smell of his pipe, so he quickly lit it to keep her at bay.

"Pilates is wonderful! Helps keep your lady parts nice and tight. Especially the kegels," Misty offered.

"Uh, first of all!" she said as P-money came back. "I'on need nothing to keep my shit tight!"

"Oh, cuz my stash of pills went missing last time you came by," she insinuated correctly. She was wrong about her assumption that Penny was fucking since she took the pills.

"Thanks for those! The kids at school loved them!" she dared and headed to her new room. She would have to unpack later, now she just needed a good cry.

§♠

*P*enny felt the heat when she joined her father plus one at dinner. The couple shared glances that gave hint to the mutual agreement they had come to. Misty had to throw in a mean blow job to seal the deal, but it was done. Women could actually learn a lesson from Misty. Instead of arguing back and forth, give a good blow job and ask for whatever it is.

"What?" Penny demanded when her father kept clearing his throat but never began.

"Well uh, we uh, you uh..." he fumbled so she turned to the one with the balls at the table.

"What Misty?" she shot her way. Even Mr. Manning turned to tune in.

"Well, your dad told me about your idea of attending an HBCU!" she cheered and cheesed on behalf of the idea. She used to party at a HBCU back in her younger days. That's where she perfected the head game that got her into a mansion. Sometimes she would spend a week at one of the frat houses, getting passed around like a blunt.

"Um, honey?" Mr. Manning called and waved to reel her back in. Visions of all those dark penises had her squirming in her seat.

"Yes, mmhm. We think it's a wonderful idea!" she said when she returned. "The rich history! The sports! The bands!"

"The thousands of miles from here!" Penny added as they stared each other down.

"Well, I have some friends who can help. I'll—" Mr. Manning offered but Penney's head was already shaking.

"No! I don't want to go as the rich white girl!" she decided. That was part of the problem at the last school. She just wanted to be regular.

"You won't need much money there," Misty added. Both Mister and Penny turned but she filled her mouth with food instead of the dicks that allowed her not to need much money there. She missed Black Friday where she would be stuffed with black dick like a turkey.

"I'll get a job and work my way through school just like mom did," Penelope told Misty while looking at her dad.

"Wonderful woman, she was," Mr. Manning said and sighed. The new Mrs. Manning sucked her teeth and left the table. "Suppose I better... yeah, good night."

"Good night," she said and laughed as he rushed after his wife. "My daddy is pussy whipped!"

"Don't touch me!" Misty fumed miserably when her husband joined her in the bedroom.

"I uh, I just meant..." he scrambled for excuses but gave up. The pretty, trophy wife seemed like a good idea once upon a time. Especially the spectacular blow jobs honed to a razor's edge from all those Black Fridays. Now it was just getting old. Good thing there was a prenup in place.

CHAPTER THIRTEEN

"So, what's on the agenda for today?" Mr. Manning asked when Penelope entered the kitchen to see him off like she used to do when she was young.

"Guess I'll head over to the library. Do some reading, research. Don't want to fall behind," she said. It sounded wonderful even though it wasn't true. It was what he wanted to hear so that's what she told him. In truth she was going to sell the last of the oxy she stole from her wicked stepmom. The rich girl certainly didn't need the money, but she did need the thrill.

"Sounds wonderful!" he cheered while his wife twisted her lips dubiously. Misty was close enough in age to know bullshit when she heard bullshit. All she was concerned with was the girl not hanging around her and disturbing her groove.

"See you later, dad," Penelope sang and kissed his cheek like years gone by. His jealous wife twisted her lips but held her tongue.

Misty waited until the house was empty before pulling her pipe and dropping a hit of crystal meth. She was good and high by the time the doorbell began its song to announce company. She confirmed through the monitor before hitting the button that opened the gate. She closed her robe to conceal the tanned nakedness beneath and headed down to open the door.

"Greg with cyberworld. Is Mister Manning at home?" the man from the security company asked.

"No, not at the moment," she replied with a wicked smile as her robe just happened to fall open.

"Good!" Greg agreed and stepped inside. He pulled the robe completely open and dropped to one knee like he was about to propose. He wasn't but he was about to eat some pussy.

"Speaking of good..." Misty laughed and lifted a leg to allow him to lick at her labia. She held onto his head to keep her balance as well as pull him into the pussy. She lost that balance when she bust a nut and they tumbled down to the marble floor. It was way too hard and cold to fuck on, so she pulled him up and up the stairs.

"Again?" Penelope wondered when she came back and saw the security company truck was back at the house. There were no new upgrades last time, so she knew something was up.

She used the pedestrian gate since the vehicle gate was more dramatic. So was the front door but luckily the guest suite she was regulated to have its own entrance. Penelope entered and followed the hisses and moans up the steps.

Misty had the mansion to herself so there was no need to lock the door. She could be seen from the hallway as the help dug her out doggy style. Penelope was equal parts appalled and enthralled. There was plenty porn online, but this was live. Curiosity caused a pause as she watched.

Penelope was a lot of different things and a virgin was one

of them. She had let a few guys eat her at school, but none got further than that. Her head tilted when he flipped her over and hoisted one leg onto his shoulders.

She winced in wonder and wondered if it hurt getting pounded like that. She had secretly watched her roommate have sex with her boyfriend while they thought she was sleep. That was a slow hump compared to this fast and furious fucking.

"I'm coming!" Greg announced. That sent the woman scrambling to get him in her mouth. No way she could explain a baby to her sterile husband.

Penelope's heart broke watching her stepmom gulp down the security man's seeds. She couldn't tell her father this. No way, so she crept away as stealthily as she had crept up. Her new mission was to get miserable Misty out of the house.

"Huh?" Misty asked when she thought she heard a footstep. Her hearing was sharp since she was so used sneak fucking and sucking her whole life.

"I didn't say anything?" Greg replied and went for his pants. He dug out a bag of pills as she looked into the monitor on the nightstand.

"Little bitch!" she growled when she saw Penelope easing back out of the house.

"Game on!" both Penelope and Misty announced as the plotting began.

❧

"What?" Mr. Manning asked when he sensed the heat flowing around the dinner table.

"Nothing!" they both declared with pasted smiles before turning back to glaring at each other.

"Had a big lunch?" Penelope asked when Misty picked at her salad.

"Bigger than normal," she shot back when she realized she wasn't going to tell her father. She may not give a fuck about the man's feelings, but his daughter sure did. "Wonderful protein shake to wash it down!"

"Yeah, but don't drink too much. They could pull the rug from under you," she warned ominously. Penelope abruptly stood and stormed off before she went too far.

"Well," Mr. Manning nodded approvingly since he was clueless to most of what his wife and daughter said most of the time.

"Are we still going to Vegas, or what?" Misty demanded. Her husband didn't want to go now that Penelope was home. She didn't have the best record of being left home alone. Still, the "or what" worried him. It usually meant a booty boycott which defeated marrying her in the first place.

"I guess we could?" he asked to see if the latest pussy embargo had ended.

"Yay! Come on Mister..." Misty cheered and led him to their bedroom like a sheep to slaughter which was exactly what she had planned for the man. The prenup may have shut her out in case of divorce but had nothing to do with life insurance.

§

"Now Penelope..." Mr Manning sighed. If he had a dollar for every time he gave this speech to his daughter he would be even richer than he was.

"Yes, father?" she asked and batted her eyes. Misty rolled hers since she used that same trick on the man all the time. Except she added a blow job with hers and got whatever she wanted out of him. She recently and literally sucked a new corvette right out his dick. That's a lot of suction.

"Misty and I are going away for the weekend. I know you leave for school Monday but still..."

"No parties. I know," she finished since she heard it plenty of times before. None of those times stopped her from actually having a party though. This one wouldn't either. "I, Penelope Manning, solemnly swear not to throw a party!"

"Well, okay then," Mr. Manning agreed since she swore and all. Penelope would keep her vow not to throw a party. P-money on the other hand made no such assurances.

"I left my pills on the counter, so you don't have to search," Misty said over her shoulder as they walked out. The young women shot each other a bird as they departed.

P-money's page had been temporarily suspended after the fiasco at school but that was easily solved by a click. Likes and DMs started popping in immediately once she posted, *"Party with P-money"*. The post went semi viral and was shared by a few semi celebs. A blast from the not so distant past popped on her phone.

"Sarah?" Penelope asked since the former BFFs hadn't spoken since going to different schools. Sarah went Ivy league back east while she stayed in state. Both had been home for the summer but hadn't connected, yet.

"Hey Penny! Or should I say, P-money!" the girl said in her best ethnic voice. It was still pretty vanilla but whatever.

"P-money for tonight bitch!" she shot back even though she had every intention of leaving that alter ego right here in sunny California. P-money would not be heading to Atlanta college with her next week.

"So, I hear you're having a party?" Sarah said, looking at the virtually viral post. "What do you need me to bring?"

"Nothing! Not even a bikini! We're going to turn up like

we used to!" she replied. An hour later the caterers and alcohol trucks rolled in. The DJ came and got set up as well. By the time nightfall fell the backyard was a full-fledged party. The former best friends hugged heartily when they reunited for the first time since the last time.

"Cool party!" Sarah shouted over the music.

"I don't know half of these people!" Penelope laughed. It didn't matter since they knew P-money. Pills were popped, shots were shot, and a noxious cloud of mixed drugs hovered above. Plus, somebody was bound to end up pregnant from all the sex acts happening all over the house.

This was the last hoorah before school and P-money planned to go as plain Penny. The turn down required a turn up, so she partied the night away. None of her personalities particularly cared for drugs harder than weed so she smoked and drank herself into a coma. The party raged on long after she crawled to her bed.

"Huh?" Penelope asked when the sexual rocking of her bed jolted her awake. What was particularly distressing was not recalling granting anyone permission to her P-hive. She bolted out the bed only to find Sarah getting a special delivery of back shots on her bed.

"Oh, hey. Good, mor, morning!" Sarah grunted in rhythm with the thrust. The Latino man making the delivery just nodded his "sup" and kept on pumping. He actually stumbled across the party by accident and came in.

"Um, why don't I give you some privacy!" she said since they didn't pause. She nearly posed the question of why her bed but found the answer when she stepped out of her room. There were couples and threesomes everywhere she looked.

The DJ was still spinning and dancing along with the people still on the floor. It came as no surprise when the cops came knocking. The presence of the police car pulling in sent a panic throughout the party. Drugs rained like confetti in an effort to get them off their persons.

"Can I speak to Penelope Manning?" an officer asked after reading the name from his notepad.

"I'm sorry officer. I'm shutting it down now!" she vowed. The cop just blinked since that didn't answer his question. "I'm Penelope."

"Is there somewhere we can speak?" he asked and looked around since they were not alone

"My, no," she almost offered her bedroom but remembered it was in use. The steady flow of people rushing out gave them the privacy he needed.

"Is your father one Robert Manning?" he asked from the pad once again.

"Yes, but he isn't here and doesn't need to know about this," she offered with a smile while mentally counting how much cash she had on hand. She usually had a couple thousand stashed around the room. He could get it all if they could keep her dad from knowing. The thoughts caused her to miss what he said so she asked, "What did you just say?"

"I regret to inform you that your father was shot in Las Vegas. A robbery gone...Shit!" the cop said and sighed when the girl passed out.

❧

"She's awake!" Sarah declared when Penelope blinked awake.

"That was some party!" Penelope declared. Had to be since she awoke with people looking down at her. Plus, she remembered a cop before she passed out. She looked around but didn't see any officers around. The house was trashed but no police.

"I'm so sorry!" Sarah whined and hugged her neck. Penelope grew concerned about the damage. She hasn't certainly caused thousands of dollars' worth of damage in previous parties, "Your dad was so sweet!"

"Was?" she asked before the notification came rushing back to mind. "Oh no! Everyone out!"

"You heard the woman! Everyone, out!" the Latino man with Sarah proclaimed and ushered the hangers on off the property. That meant waking a few up and shutting the DJ down. He was rolling off so many different drugs there was no telling how long he would have played.

"Uh, you too um..." Penelope said and turned to Sarah for his name.

"I don't know," she shrugged and ushered him out next. "Call me..."

"Misty did this! Whatever happened, she did it!" she declared even before getting the facts. The fact that she was a conniving cheater was enough for her.

CHAPTER FOURTEEN

*T*hings went from bad to worse when Penelope made it out to Vegas. Sarah's dad whisked her there immediately to get to the bottom of this. Misty still hadn't called her but was there at the police station when they arrived.

"What happened to my father, you tramp!" she shouted and had to be refrained. Good thing too because Penelope Manning had never been in a fist fight in her life. Misty grew up in trailer parks and alleys. She would have whooped her ass to add injury to insult.

"Someone tried to rob us. My Robert saved me!" Misty wept without shedding a tear. Kinda like Kyle Rittenhouse when he was on trial.

"Yes, we have had a rash of robberies in the area," the robbery detective admitted.

"Good, can I have the death certificate so I can process the insurance policies?" Misty asked greedily.

"Uh, he's in a coma, not dead," he said and she stormed out.

"She has something to do with this!" Penelope promised.

"That wouldn't be a first," the cop admitted. Now he had to prove it. The pending investigation would hold up any insurance payouts until completed.

"You're welcome to stay at the house with us," Sarah's dad offered as they headed back to the car.

"I'm leaving for school in a few days!" Sarah reminded her.

"That's fine. Your mom and I—" he was saying but Penelope cut in.

"There's nothing I can do but wait. I may as well go to school until then," she said and sighed.

The pending cases froze the insurance policies, but Misty had access to the household account. It wasn't the millions she had hoped for but enough to shop and party on in the interim. Meanwhile, Penelope had to live on the money in her own accounts. Luckily for her it was more than some grownups make in a year.

Enough to fly out to Atlanta and attend the HBCU, Atlanta College. She insisted on not being the rich white girl, so she signed up to live in the dorms. She was assigned a four-person room in the Frederick Ferguson Female center. An all-girls dorm affectionately known as the FFF. Or as the guys called it, fuck for food since quite a few of the incoming freshmen would do just that.

The dorm housed underprivileged girls from all across the state and country. Penelope left her Benz out west and planned to live off the land like any other sophomore would. Being first to arrive gave her first dibs on the four bunks spread around the room. She opted for the bed next to the window just in case her roommates had hygiene issues.

"Well, I didn't quite think that through..." Penelope mused when she began to unpack. She was trying to downplay her affluence, but all the designer labels contradicted her. She shook her head and continued to unpack since her new room-mates were on the way.

&.

"Welcome to Atlanta!" Callie cheered as she read the sign on the highway. Each state was a celebration since she knew she would never live in New York city again. She never met the family she left behind along with the bad memories.

There were good memories as well and watching KT and Slime get murdered was near the top of the list. The splat of brain matter on the building put a smile on her face as she navigated through her new city. The GPS guided her right to her new home.

"Frederick Ferguson Female Center?" she read from the sign but was confused by all the men milling about. Mainly upperclassmen hoping to fuck first. The building would soon fill with future lawyers, doctors and assorted movers and shakers but these black men just wanted to be first to put their dick in them.

"Need help with yo' bags, shawty?" a male student asked as soon as she opened her door.

"A-yo son, beat it!" she shot back forcefully and clutched the bag containing the life savings her man lost his life over. She intended to put it in the bank but held it close until then.

"Say word?" a fellow New Yorker cheered when he heard the accent. He saw the license plates and diddy bopped over.

"Fuck outa here, B!" Callie barked and shot him down as well. She gripped her money bag and another and headed up to her assigned room. She walked in not knowing what to expect, especially not a white girl talking to herself.

"Penny, Penelope, P-money..." she debated as to what to

go by with her new roommates. She ran out of time since the first of them had arrived. Penelope shrugged her shoulders and decided to let them decide. "Hey, I'm Penelope but you can call me Penny, or P-money?"

"Penny!" Callie decided quickly. "I'm Callie."

"Callie from New York!" Penny cheered happily, easily picking up on her accent.

"Word. So, we just pick a bed?" she asked as she looked around the room. Each bed had its own dresser and desk assigned. The drawers had a latch to add padlocks for extra security.

"Sure, unless you want this one? I can unpack and—"

"Look, white girl. I mean, Penny," Callie began. "I'm not sure why you decided to come to this particular school but, stand firm. Don't be a pushover or people gonna push you over!"

"Gotcha!" Penny agreed. She had never seen the ugly side of life but her new roommate had. Callie was street savvy enough to know she wasn't at all. But Callie was here by herself, that was all the looking out she had to give.

🐌

"*P*lay a number 'fo yo' granny 'fo you go?" Zenobia's grandmother asked and sipped her forty of the hood's finest malt liquor.

"You waited too late. I gotta go!" she replied and kissed the woman's sweaty face before hitting the door. She moved too quickly and forgot to hold her breath and got a nostril full of her pissy smell. All that malt liquor made for a lot of peeing and she didn't always make it to the bathroom.

"Okay, baby. You have fun at that there school," she said and sighed.

"I'm not going for fun. I—okay, granny," she replied and stopped short of correcting her. The old lady had taken her in once she lost everything in the fire. She got another dose of the p funk when she leaned in for another kiss.

Zenobia lost her car, clothes and memories in the fire but luckily, she had a nice nest egg from the prison hustle. Her father bought her another car from prison, so she packed her new clothes and shoes for her new life. Even though she was a sophomore this would be her first time in the dorm so she was assigned to the FFF, as well.

Assigned parking gave students one less thing to fight about, even though they would find plenty other things to fight about. She noticed a man leaned back with his eyes closed in a parked car in one of the spots assigned to her room.

"Damn!" Zenobia when she saw the top of a blue wig bobbing up and down in his lap. She thought she was escaping junkies turning tricks in plain sight by coming to college. It was every day on her old block, so she treated this like she treated those and ignored it.

"Need some help, Miss Lady?" a chubby junior asked when he spotted her taking her bags from the trunk.

"Sure," she accepted but he got sidetracked by the blow job in the next car. By the time he looked up again, she had already lugged her luggage inside. She found her room and used the key to enter.

"You can't have the window bed!" Penny declared, causing Callie to shake her head. She told her not to be a pushover, but that didn't mean being a dork either.

"You go to Atlanta college?" Zenobia asked with her face twisted up to show what she thought of it.

"Yes! Plenty of Caucasian, Asian and people of Latino

descent attend historically black—" Penny was explaining but obviously ran out of time.

"Hey, girl. I'm Zenobia. You can call me Z!" she introduced Callie while Penny kept right on with her spiel.

Callie knew then she liked the white girl, and that Zenobia didn't like white people. Which was odd since they were nearly the same complexion. Penny kept right on talking as the door opened once more and in walked their fourth roommate with her bags.

"Hey y'all! I'm Michaela. After my daddy. From Chi town..." she rattled off in one long clip. Callie didn't want to be quick to judge but was pretty sure she wasn't going to like her. Her eyes shot in every direction while she spoke. Like scoping everything and everyone.

"Well, that's the last bed! I'm Penny!" Penny greeted. Meanwhile, Zenobia tilted her head curiously at her blue hair.

"Shoot! I'm late. I was down in the parking lot paying for my ride," the newcomer explained, which explained where Zenobia saw her before.

"Ewww," Zenobia grimaced and began to unpack. The rest resumed putting their belongings away in their new home.

"Need me a shower after that long ass bus ride!" Michaela grunted and looked around.

"There," Penny said and pointed at the small bathroom they would share.

"Thanks," she replied and began to strip right there, on the spot. Zenobia turned away while Callie looked, like 'what the fuck'.

"Cool tat!" Penny cheered of the bullseye tattooed on each ass cheek.

"Hell yeah, birth control!" Michaela laughed. The confused looks made her laugh harder before explaining.

"Niggas don't like to use rubbers, so I let them aim at the bullseye."

"Ewww!" Z repeated and grimaced.

"I gotta make a run!" Callie said when she looked at the time. Banks would be closing soon so she had to handle her business. Michaela had looked at the bag with her money too many times for comfort. It was more than her life savings, it cost her man his life.

"I'm next in the shower!" Penny called, then punked out. "Unless you want next?"

"Girl..." Z fussed and rolled her eyes. She didn't like Michaela and hated the white girl. Callie seemed cool, so this was going to be interesting.

♞

"$\mathcal{I}$ brought burgers!" Callie cheered and held a bag of food in the air as she returned to the room.

"Thanks! I was just about to order something!" Penny cheered.

"How much is mine? I'll pay for it," Z stated plainly. She hadn't been on the planet very long but long enough to know nothing is free.

"Nine bucks then!" Callie snapped. She was trying to be nice but could be just as mean if she wanted to be. Zenobia handed her a ten and got a dollar change.

"I already ate, but thanks," Michaela said as she accepted the free meal.

"Ewww," Zenobia grimaced again when she recalled seeing the girl eating a dick. Callie could finally relax since her money was safely tucked away in her bank account. They ate in silence before she showered and got into her bed.

"Whaaaat! You going to sleep already? All these parties!" Michaela demanded and danced in place.

"I just drove fourteen hours. Hell yeah, I'm going to bed!" she shot back. Michaela looked around the room to see if her other roommates were game. They weren't, which was fine by her.

"Let me blaze up before I go shake this ass!" Michaela announced and pulled out half a blunt. "Y'all smoke?"

Penny smoked occasionally but reserved judgement to see what the other girls had to say. She wasn't sure if Callie or Zenobia was the boss. She just knew she wasn't.

"Have you read the rule book? No male company, no drugs, no..." Z read verbatim from the rule book.

"So?" Michaela shrugged as she searched for her lighter. Some people don't care about rules, and she was one of them.

"So, light it and we fighting!" Callie said, pulling her blanket back so she could get up. She had nowhere else to go and wasn't letting someone else get her kicked out.

"I like to fight." Michaela laughed and kept on searching for her lighter.

"Good, cuz you finna have to fight both of us," Zenobia added calmly even though she was anything but calm. She too wasn't letting anything stand in her way. Plus, she didn't want to go back to her grandmother's pissy house.

"Y'all some lames!" Michaela declared and stormed off.

"I was um... with you guys!" Penny nodded once the girl was gone.

"Shut up, white girl." Zenobia laughed and shook her head. She wanted to hate her for being white, but Penny wasn't her mother. Especially when they both heard her whimpers all night. They both knew the pain of losing some-one. None knew it would be the glue that bonded them.

CHAPTER FIFTEEN

"*J* got first!" Penny proclaimed when the alarm clocks began to buzz around the room. "Unless you guys wanna go?"

"Use the bathroom, white girl!" Zenobia fussed. Penny grabbed her toiletries and rushed into the bathroom.

"You can go next." Zenobia offered across the room.

"How much you gonna charge me?"'Callie asked sarcastically. She felt some kinda way about being rebuffed while trying to treat her roommates to dinner.

"Ha, ha," Zenobia fake laughed in surrender. "Thanks for dinner. You can give my money back if it makes you feel better."

"Nah," she laughed. Z laughed too until they both noticed the empty bed. Both heads began to shake since today would be a particularly busy day.

Incoming students had a full day of seminars, orientation and education. The school went to great lengths to give the students every opportunity to succeed. A part of educating kids from the hood is unlearning all the filth they learned in the hood. And in the broken homes and foster homes. Even a financial class to help manage the meager stipend they gave out.

The twenty-five bucks a week was given to augment the room and board. It was plenty for pads, Ramen noodles and a snack and a half. But if they bought weed or alcohol pills or partied it wouldn't last 'til Tuesday.

They shrugged her absence off since it wasn't their problem. Each girl had enough of their own problems to keep them busy. Penny finished her shower and relinquished the bathroom. Callie and Zenobia nodded at each other, so Callie hopped up and took the offer. The three girls moved in the synchronized manner needed to share the same space. They almost forgot there was a fourth.

"Hey y'all! Whew!" Michaela swooned when she stumbled into the room moments before the rest were ready to leave. She smelled like alcohol, smoke and sex from the festivities.

"How was the party?" Penny asked eagerly.

"Girl, that shit was lit! Err drug you want and..." she paused to burp and grimace. "Don't you hate when you burp and can taste the dick you sucked earlier?'

"Um, no?" Penny replied on her own behalf and looked at the others. Their screwed up faces said they hadn't either. "Taste like hot dog, but I never..."

"Ewww," both Callie and Zenobia frowned.

"Y'all ain't never sucked no dick? Let me find out y'all like coochie! Cuz I'm with that too!" she called after them as they headed out. She had the same meetings as they did but still crawled into bed for some much needed sleep.

"I give her a month," Callie guessed as they stepped out into the brilliant Atlanta sunshine.

"I was thinking a week," Zenobia countered.

"Bet?" she said, extending a pinky. They twisted their pinkies to confirm the bet. Zenobia furrowed her brow when she saw what Penny was wearing.

"Yeah she fly," Callie said when she saw what she was looking at.

"Knock off," Penny shot back. She intended to downplay her affluence by dressing down but her dressing down was still all designer labels.

"Okay, knock off." Callie laughed knowingly. She knew the difference between real and bootleg but if that's what she wanted to sell, she would buy it.

"Anyways, lunch on me today girls," Penny declared as they neared the building. The next few hours were dedicated to surviving in an HBCU.

§⚫

"*I*'m just in time!" Michaela cheered when she entered the student center. The dining hall was included in the room and board, but no one really wanted to eat the food. Rumor had it that it came from the county jail to save money. Luckily, S&S brands had set up a discount burger joint. It was there to employ students who needed extra money to survive, instead of making a profit.

"Mmp," Zenobia huffed but held her tongue. When she placed her order along with theirs.

"So, what I missed?" the latecomer asked and got an eye roll from Z.

"Uh, orientation," Callie said, shaking her head.

"Oh, they said...." the helpful white girl said and filled her in verbatim. Michaela still didn't pay much attention as she scanned the room.

"Ooh, that's the dude I spent the night with," Michaela

whispered when a guy walked by with his friends. He looked over her as if he had never seen her before in this, or any other life.

"Hmph," Zenobia repeated.

"Shoot, I should fill out an application?" Callie asked, seeking advice. The money in the bank would dwindle if she didn't augment it with income. After years of being a dope boy's girlfriend she needed a little bit more than twenty-five dollars a week.

"I may too," Zenobia cosigned. It was settled so they headed back to the counter to fill them out once they finished lunch.

"Shoot, I know where we can make a hundred bucks a day without flipping damn burgers!" Michaela hissed as if flipping burgers was beneath her. Truth be told, flipping burgers is as honorable as any other profession.

"What, dancing?" Penny asked and scrunched her face to let her know what she thought about that idea. Even girls from her expensive school were stripping on the side.

"Hell naw! Too much work! We can get paid doing the same shit we do err damn day," Michaela said and sold her on the idea.

"Okay, I'm down," Penny nodded as the other girls started back to the table.

"I'll put you on girl," she whispered like it was their little secret. In Penny's old world, most secrets were secret because they were no good. This new world wasn't much different than where she came from. "Let me hold a twenty."

"ou look cute!" Callie cheered and tried not to laugh when Zenobia came out of the bathroom in her uniform.

"Oh, this came for you while you was out," Z replied and shot her a bird. The two were getting closer while Penny still tried to please everyone. Zenobia still held a grudge about something Penny could never make up for.

"Welp." Callie sighed and went to change into her S&S uniform, as well. Michaela was the only one who would change right in the middle of the room. Callie and Zenobia would always turn away while Penny peeped out more of her tats. Including several names crossed out and covered up.

"You think that white girl really got some bread?" Zenobia asked as they headed off to their shift at the burger joint.

"Think? I know!" Callie proclaimed. Her clothes and mannerisms all spelled more money than she was pretending not to have. Little did they know her father's assets were still frozen in legal limbo as he still hovered between this world and the next.

"Ooh, girl, can I wear your Prada?" Michaela pleaded as soon as they were alone.

"Um... I... um... okay?" Penny guessed since the girl was a couple sizes thicker in the hips.

"Thanks!" she squealed and peeled off her jeans. Penny tilted her head curiously when she saw the girl was already wearing a pair of her panties. Especially since they had to come from the hamper since she had just worn them. They fit differently on her with her round, brown ass cheeks hanging from the bottom. Michaela saw her looking and nodded. "Let me find out!"

"I'll get an Uber," Penny said and turned away. She was

missing her car already, but the new Benz was way too much, too much around here. A few students drove the same model but none lived in the dorm. There were quite a few students from families of means who just wanted to attend the same school their parents attended. Some parents even met here and married.

Michaela rambled on about things Penny never heard of in life. Mainly about the gang life of her native Chicago and all the violence she witnessed. Penny realized she had been handicapped by her upbringing just as much as hers gave her an advantage. The only question now was how she would fare in this new environment. Finding this good paying job was a good start.

"Here we are!" she announced when they arrived. She had already worked a few shifts before getting a booth for her roommate.

"Oh, okay?" Penny wondered aloud as they wandered inside. It was dimly lit but she noticed cubicle-like booths running along both walls.

"*N*umber eight," a man said, handing out assignments to the men and women in the line. Penny was next so she got, "Number nine."

"What did you say we had to do?" Penny questioned again as they headed to their stations.

"Same thing we been doing. Shoot I been doing it since I was twelve!" she said and disappeared into her booth.

Penny shrugged and entered her own booth. She expected a desk, phone, computer maybe but there was none. Nothing but a swivel chair so she sat. That's when she noticed the round holes in each side of the booth. Her head tilted curiously as she leaned in to get a look through the hole and nearly got poked in the eye.

"The fuck?" she said and wondered at the object that entered the hole. It took a second to realize it was a dick and she smacked it away. Except that only made it get hard. Penny was so infuriated she grabbed it with both hands and pulled. She ended up with both feet on the wall as she pulled with all of her might.

"Aghhh!" the owner of the dick howled for help before his dick was disjointed.

"What the hell are you doing?" the man who passed out stations asked when he snatched the door open.

Penny didn't have time to explain, so she let go and took off. She forgot all about a ride and ran all the way back to the dorm.

🍃

"Wait..." Callie began as she tried to make sense of what the hysterical girl was saying. Zenobia heard it correctly the first time and was beet red from laughing so hard. Callie noticed that they shared the same shade of crimson for someone who didn't like white people. "What?"

"A dick! It came through the hole!" Penny shouted. "It was this big!"

"Ouch!" Zenobia laughed at the two-foot-long dick she made with her hands.

"That's just nasty," Callie decided and shook her head. She was complaining about making French fries for the last few hours but at least no one stuck their dick in her face. They were still going on when Michaela returned from her shift.

"Girl, you lame as fuck!" she snapped at Penny. Callie

almost intervened but Z waved her off to see what Penny would do.

"Me? No, you! "she shouted back and stood. "You didn't tell me you worked in a damn, damn—"

"Glory hole," Zenobia offered but only because she googled it.

"I ain't tell you I didn't!" Michaela shot back in her defense.

"That don't make sense?" Callie said as she wondered about her response.

"Anyway. More for me," she said as she changed tunes. She may have lost out on the referral fee, but did double up on dick and made some extra money. "Y'all not coming to the party?"

"No, but only cuz it's Tuesday and we're in college," Zenobia quipped but sarcasm requires a degree of intelligence to be perceived. Michaela's had been dumbed down by drugs and alcohol.

"More for me!" She shrugged again. "Time y'all jump off the porch, y'all gonna get my leftovers!"

"What does that even mean?" Penny asked. She was plenty hip and very smart but that one got past her.

"Means she finna fuck the whole city of Atlanta," Z answered correctly. If the whole city lined up, she would certainly fuck them.

"Wait..." Callie laughed when she suddenly recalled something else Penny relayed. Zenobia started laughing already even though she didn't know what she found funny.

"Yes?" Penny twisted her lips since none of it was funny to her yet.

"You said there were dudes there too?" she asked and laughed some more.

"Welcome to Atlanta, chile. Dudes will suck dick and lick

ass but not eat pussy!" Z said sorrowfully. The revelation put an end to the long day, and everyone retired to their pillow.

"Good night, Callie, Z!" Penny called through the dark.

"Go to sleep, white girl!" Zenobia shot back. Penny cracked a smile since she knew she was wearing her down. They would be friends whether she liked it or not.

CHAPTER SIXTEEN

"*Y*ou wanna take a ride with me?" Zenobia asked.

"Sure!" Penny agreed and stood.

"Yeah, but no I'm talking to her boo-boo," Z snipped. Callie just shook her head and stifled a laugh.

"Can't. Gotta study," she said and sighed. It was a lovely Saturday afternoon, and she would have loved to get out and see more of her new city but her new classes demanded her full attention.

"Me! Me! Ooh me!" Penny exclaimed, pointing at her raised hand.

"Girl come on!" Z groaned like it was killing her to be nice. All she could do was laugh at the white girl's twerk celebration. "Okay, I'ma need you to never do that again!"

"Never, ever!" Callie added and dove back into her studies. She didn't even register when they left the room.

"Where we headed?" Penny asked as buckled her seatbelt. She got a side eye for a reply. "Oh."

"I gotta see my granny," Zenobia replied. Just because she

was in a hurry to get out of there didn't mean she didn't have to check on her. She still hadn't built the nerve to go back down to the prison to see her father. Sexual abuse takes a lot out of a person.

Penny saw Zenobia go inside her own head and took the opportunity to do the same. There had been no answers in her father's shooting and his finances were still frozen. She knew it was just a matter of time before she was totally alone in the world.

"Your granny?" Penny asked of the old lady on the front porch as they pulled into the driveway.

"In the flesh," she said. She was just about to make a silent prayer that granny didn't do anything embarrassing but you have to pray quicker with this granny.

"Hey now!" the woman cheered and tried to get up a little too quickly. She slipped, tripped and landed on her back but didn't spill one sip of her malt liquor. She leaned up and took a big swig as they rushed to help.

"Oh my gosh. Are you okay?" Penny gushed but Zenobia was a little more reserved since she had been through this a time a two before.

"Anitra?" the old lady squinted up at Penny. She went for her glasses, but they couldn't see through the drink.

"No, this ain't no Anitra!" Z fussed as they helped her up. Once she was right side up, she nodded that the woman hadn't come back from the dead. Plus, they didn't favor much besides the lack of melanin.

"Y'all hungry? I cooked," the old lady offered and attempted to get up again.

"Sure!" Penny was saying to be polite until she registered the look on Zenobia's face. It usually accompanied one of her "Ewwws", so she shook her head. "Sure aren't. Thanks, but..."

"I feel lucky today! Run and get my numbers?" granny pleaded.

"I got you," she said like old times. And just like old times she knew what came next and beat her to it. "And a forty ounce!"

"Your grandmother is cool! Mines was all stuffy like the Queen of England," Penny recalled.

"Probably looks like the Queen too," Z laughed, but not for long.

"She did. She's dead now," she shot back and twisted her lips.

"I'm sorry! My bad!" she offered apologetically.

"I'm lying. Just wanted to crack your face!" Penny laughed.

"Crack yo' dang face!" Z laughed even more as she pulled into the ghetto strip mall. Her face changed by the time she put the car in park and reached over for the glove box. A picture fell out as she pulled a box cutter from under her paperwork and looked at the pack of girls looking at her.

"Who is this?" Penny asked as she looked at the smiling white lady in the picture.

"Nobody!" she shot back and put the picture back before looking back at the girls. "Stay here!"

"Okay!" Penny agreed because those girls looked rough. She hit the locks just like a white lady once Zenobia headed to the store. She tilted her head back and walked right through the gathering.

"I know this bitch didn't!" one declared while another added, "After what her police ass brother did!"

Zenobia second guessed her decision to come inside instead of just driving off. Anitra wasn't the best mother, but she didn't raise no punk. Not in a daughter anyway because she now had beef because of her punk ass brother.

"Hey, lil sister! Haven't seen you in a while?" the middle eastern clerk cheered when he saw the once regular customer. So regularly he started for the lottery machine for her numbers.

"I went away to college," she replied and cheesed broadly at how wonderful it sounded.

"Good for you. This place not for you," he said with a grimace and shook his head. He rang up her numbers but waved off the beer, knowing it wasn't for her.

"No. This place is not for me," she agreed and looked to the pack of girls waiting for her to come back out. She let out a sigh knowing her granny might not get her forty. Nope, it might end up upside one of these chick's head.

"Here she come!" one said and her work was done. She had instigated the rest and stepped aside.

"Excuse me," Zenobia said just so she knew she tried to be peaceful. She gripped the bottle like a club in case they didn't want peace.

"Fuck you mean, 'scruse me!" the leader said. She obviously wasn't selected for her pronunciation since the word "excuse" just whipped her ass.

"Look, I'on want no smoke. Just tryna get my granny a beer," she reasoned quite reasonably.

"Fuck yo' granny when yo' snitching ass brother got Carlos kilt!" another girl cosigned. The pack of rats inched forward as she gripped the box cutter in her pocket. A spark was all this volatile situation needed, and here it came.

"Oh hell naw! Fuck y'all hoes tryna do?" Penny barked and provided the spark as she got out of the car she was told to stay inside of. "P-money out this bih!"

The gang of girls looked so confused by the gangsta ass white girl they froze in place. Most of the white girls who came through here were junkies, but this one was with the shit. The novelty quickly wore off and a girl swung on Zenobia. She dipped the blow and popped her in the head with the bottle. It was about to be a full-fledged melee until someone fired a gun.

"That's enough!" the store clerk shouted with his smoking pistol in the air. "Break it up and go home!"

The reprieve allowed Zenobia and Penny time to get to the car and pull off. She chirped away and skidded around corners back to her grandmother's house. Neither said a word until they pulled back into the driveway.

"Are you crazy?" Z needed to know. Penny twisted her lips like she was trying to figure that part out.

"Me, no. P-money is tho!" She laughed and raised a hand for a high five. A high five takes another hand though and Zenobia had left her hanging. She shook her head and got out to deliver the goods so they could go back to school.

"My mom," Zenobia said when she got back into the car. Penny looked confused by the random statement, so Zenobia pulled the same picture from the glove box again. They were officially friends now, so she explained. "*Her.* She's my mom."

&

"Uh-oh! What's this?" Callie asked when Z and Penny came into the room cackling like friendly hens with shiny new eggs to sit on.

"Girl, why you ain't tell me about P-money?" Zenobia howled.

"Oh Lawd! I thought I told you not to tell nobody about that name?" Callie laughed.

"We was about to rumble in da hood!" Penny cheered and

laughed along with her friends. "And I ain't never had a fight in my life!"

"Wait, what?" Z reeled in disbelief. Those were some rough street chicks. "They would have snatched every strand of hair from your head. Sewed it in and wore it to the club!"

"That's rough!" Callie agreed and on cue walked Michaela.

"Let me hold ten dollars?" she asked as she entered. Her lips twisted like Bobby and Whitney as she waited. She just tossed the question in the air so anyone could answer. Only one did.

"Here," Penny said and dug into her purse. She only had a twenty, so she instructed, "Bring me my change!"

"Mmhm," Michaela hummed and rushed from the room.

"Let me hold a ten. I'll bring you back yo' change," Callie quipped.

"Me too!" Zenobia laughed.

"While y'all playing. Owing me ten will keep her from asking for a few days," Penny explained.

"And when she do ask, you finna give it to her again!" Z fussed. They were friends now and she was protective of her friends. Even from themselves.

"She'll steal if I don't," she snarled. Trinkets and items had been coming up missing more and more.

"Don't tell me that's where my watch went!" Callie demanded. She had accepted misplacing it, or having lost it. She would not, could not accept it being stolen. She had lost everything once and was slowly getting her possessions back.

"Girl, I'm missing panties and bras from my hamper?" Zenobia wondered aloud. At first she thought she was tripping because who steals dirty clothes? The banter died when the door opened and in walked the devil.

"Hey, y'all!" Michaela cheered and wobbled her way in.

She let out a loud, deep burp that filled the air with the smell of malt liquor and semen. She looked around for a reply but got the same shocked look from all. She looked dramatically different than when they all arrived a couple months ago. "Can I borrow ten bucks?"

"What happened to your job?" Zenobia asked since she was bumming more than usual lately.

"Man, they fired my ass! Talmbout, I was burning," she said and shook her head along with the other shaking heads. "So, I need ten bucks."

"Hell naw! I—" Z began but Penny cut in before she could finish.

"Here," Penny said and came off another twenty. Callie twisted her lips dubiously. Penny was playing poor white girl yet had a steady stream of cash to go along with her designer labels. Meanwhile, Michaela took off like she had been shot out of a cannon.

"How you gonna keep giving her money?" Zenobia fussed.

"Plus, you know she gone be right back asking for more!" Callie added while Penny smiled mischievously.

"Or stealing," Penny said and laid another ten on her bed. She silently explained when she angled her laptop at the bed. There was a ton of porn online from this same angle, but she was trying to catch a thief.

"And we finna beat that bitch ass when we catch her!" Z proclaimed since that would be proof she stole everything else that was missing around here.

"Nah, we gonna show the Dean and get her ass kicked out the room!" Penny said. She would know since her last Dean put her out of her last college.

"Yeah, so we don't get in trouble ourselves," Callie nodded. The rule book clearly stated all students involved in physical altercations would be expelled from the dorm. Zenobia would rather whoop the girl but acquiesced with her friends.

The trap was set, now all they had to do was wait for the rat to come take the bait.

CHAPTER SEVENTEEN

"And, action!" Penny announced when the laptop alerted movement in the dorm room. The girls all huddled around the screen from a booth at S&S burgers.

"How much more evidence do we need?" Zenobia hissed. "We already got her stealing the ten!"

"That's just ten. The Dean might tell us to let it go," Callie said. All heads tilted when Michaela pulled a pipe from her bra, then a rock from her sock.

"That should get it!" Penny laughed as the sizzling sound came through, loud and clear.

"Bruh, we got a whole crackhead in the room with us," Z said, shaking her head. It really wasn't funny, but they all laughed.

The trio had become a crew and it was time to drop the dead weight. They were midway through the semester which meant they wouldn't get a replacement roommate once they got rid of Michaela. It would just be them until summer break. The heads tilted to the other side when Michaela got up and started dancing.

"That's electric crackhead!" Zenobia chuckled as she gave the dance a name.

"Un-uh, she doing the pop-rock!" Callie added and laughed at her own joke.

"That's the petrologist!" Penny cracked up louder and longer until she realized no one laughed with her. Instead, they twisted their lips. "It's the—"

"Study of rocks!" both replied before she could finish.

"We got it. It just wasn't funny," Callie explained. They would have laughed some more but onscreen Michaela demanded their attention.

"What the fuck is she doing!" Callie wondered aloud when Michaela lifted the lid on her hamper and dug in. They watched as she pulled a pair of panties, held it to her nose and inhaled.

"Looking for mushrooms," Zenobia cackled.

"My box smells like a box of fresh cut roses!" she shot back.

"Mine is a box of chocolate!" Penny declared and got side eyed. "White chocolate?"

"Sometimes you just gotta not say nothing," Zenobia patronized and patted her hand.

"This is one of them sometimes," Callie added. They were busy joking while Michaela was loading up. She went around to each hamper and stole underclothes, socks and jeans. She tugged at the lock on each drawer before giving up... Almost.

"No! Don't!" Penny shouted as Michaela went towards the laptop. It was too little too late because she snapped it closed and tucked it under her arm.

The girls rushed back to the dorm, but crackheads move at the speed of crack, so she was long gone. All they could do was take stock of their losses and headed over to the Dean's office. There was always a wait so they waited their turn to see the busy man.

"Dean Jenkins will see you now," the secretary announced when their turn came. She held the door to allow them to enter.

"Hello, ladies! How can I help you?" the middle-aged man asked while greedily looking like he wanted to help himself to some breast. His eyes ran back and forth between the six tits like he was a judge in a tit contest. He sucked the chicken grease from his fingers and closed the box of wings.

"Our roommate stole panties, is a crackhead, begs for money, snifs panties!" they all blurted at the same time.

"Panties? Did I hear panties?" he demanded since that was all he heard. It was all he ever heard.

"Bruh, we said a lot more than damn panties!" Penny growled.

"Chill, P," Zenobia said and squeezed her hand. She had no plans on going to live with her granny again so she couldn't afford to get kicked out.

"Look," Callie said forcefully and paused so her partners knew she had the floor. "Our roommate is using drugs in the room. She is stealing everything that isn't locked down. Clothes, money and now her laptop,"

On cue Penny presented her phone to show the video evidence. Mr. Jenkins squirmed and grunted when Michaela sniffed the panties. His head began to nod as he pulled his keyboard to type in her name.

"Michaela Victors..." he spelled as he typed. The news was etched in his face even before he began to speak. "She hasn't been to class since class began?"

The Dean furrowed his brow even deeper as he dug deeper into her records. It looked like the little crack head had slipped through the cracks. She had been withdrawn from every class for lack of attendance but was still enrolled. Only for a moment though when he called an assistant.

"Victors, Michaela," the Dean said and paused for her to get it up. "Mmhm, yes. Mmhm."

"Well?" Callie asked when he hung up but got hung up on Zenobia's chest again.

"Well what? Oh! Yes, she's been expelled. Maintenance will come to change the locks," he replied.

"What if she comes back? We don't wanna get in trouble for fighting?" Zenobia said all pouty, causing her friends to whip their heads in her direction. If they didn't know her, they would have bought the act themselves.

"Handle yo' 'biz!" he assured and grabbed a wing from the box. He sucked all the meat off of a flat as he looked at the asses leaving his office.

❧

"Good riddance!" Penny sighed as they headed back to the dorm. They ignored the steady flow of cat calls and come ons from fellow students and passersby.

"I hope the bitch comes back!" Callie huffed. She wanted to take out the New York robbery on her too.

"Word, B!" Zenobia teased in her mock New York accent.

"Oh, I know you not talking! When y'all 'ta li' thi!" Callie shot back. Penny snickered at them both and they both turned their heads at her.

"What?" she reeled. She asked and they told her.

"Like totally narly. Like, oh my God!" they both rattled in their best valley girl accents. They laughed and bantered until they reached the dorm. It all came to an end when they spotted the crack head toting a large bag from the building.

"Uh-oh..." Michaela said when she looked up and saw the trio coming towards her. Crackheads are known for their quick thinking, so she was ready. "Hey y'all! We got robbed! But I got all our stuff back. I'ma need fifty no, a hundred bucks tho."

"Okay, oh," Penny agreed. Zenobia turned to fuss at her, but she had already taken off on the crackhead.

"That must be P-money!" Callie laughed when the white girl socked the crack head in her mouth. A yellow incisor tumbled in the air from the first blow. Michaela's gums were already grey and puffy from all the crack smoke, so they had trouble holding her teeth in any way. She had just lost a molar giving a blow job earlier in the day.

"Bitch!" Michaela snarled and put up her hands. The rough girl had a mean fight game but not enough to defend the six fists coming from each direction.

She lost a few more teeth under the barrage of blows but never went down. Crack heads don't mind getting their asses whooped, but once she realized she wasn't going to get any money for crack she gave up and took off. Ain't no catching a crack head once they get up to speed. One outran a cheetah on animal planet.

"Yoooo!" That's crazy!" a guy cheered and set off a round of whoops and hollers from the crowd.

"Shit!" Penny fussed when she saw so many phones pointed in their direction. Except the ones that were already uploading the footage.

"Damn pretty thugs!" another male laughed and shook his head.

"That's what my man used to call me! His pretty thug!" Callie moaned in between sunshine and rain of the joy mixed with pain.

"Well, that's us now! The pretty thugs!" Zenobia said decided to own it instead of fighting it.

𝒷

"Uh-oh," Penny moaned when she looked at her ringing phone. She didn't know the number, but the California area code had her on edge. It could either be good news or bad news and she didn't like those odds.

"You okay? Your face is white as a ghost!" Callie reeled and crossed the room to her side. The room seemed like it had tripled in size once they got rid of the negative girl.

"Y-y-y-yeah. No, it's my dad," she managed as the phone stopped ringing. She didn't speak about her family once since arriving at school. The caller wasn't taking no answer for an answer and the phone began to ring a few seconds later.

"Want me to get it?" Z asked since she was just as protective over her friends as they were with her. Penny couldn't speak so she nodded her head and handed the phone over.

"Hello?" Zenobia asked in a tone right in the middle of "can I help you" and "get the fuck off my phone".

"Penelope Manning?" a woman asked softly. The compassion in her voice told Zenobia this wasn't good news. She put the phone on speaker and answered.

"Yes?"

"I'm sorry to inform you your dad has taken a turn for the worse. Mrs. Manning has authorized termination of life support," she revealed.

"Mrs. Manning is dead! That bitch is an imposter!" Penny pointed and shouted at the phone. The woman wasn't quite sure what to make of that so she went around it.

"We're calling all next of kin to allow goodbyes before unhooking the machines that sustain his life," she continued.

"I'm on my way!" she yelled and jumped from her bed. She had reached the door before realizing she didn't have anything for the trip. Especially what she needed most. "Will you guys come to California with me?"

"Hell yeah!" Zenobia exclaimed before Callie could speak.

"Uh, we got class!" she reminded.

"Girl, it's a week before break! We'll get our assignments online!" Zenobia reminded since that was an option. Atlanta college was a firm believer that shit happens, so they gave students every opportunity to stay up or catch up.

Callie looked at Penny's trembling hands as she tried to load clothes in a bag and the choice was clear. Even without assignments she had to help her friend. She nudged her aside and picked up the task of packing her bag before packing one of her own.

Zenobia summoned an Uber, so they wouldn't have to pay for the airport parking. She figured the last minute flights were going to cost an arm and leg, but she was wrong. They were an arm, leg and left eye. Luckily, Penny put them all on her card when they arrived at the airport.

"All they had was business class!" she fussed apologetically.

"*O*h, okay," Zenobia replied and shrugged since she had never been on a plane before.

"It'll have to do!" Zenobia exclaimed but she had never been on a plane either. Penny on the other hand was used to first class, private jets and helicopters.

"Have to do alright," Callie muttered when the business class boarded right after the first class. She noticed the first-class flyers turning their noses up at them so she made sure to pass it along when the coach passengers began to file by.

"Would you ladies like a drink before we taxi?" a stewardess asked politely.

"Champagne, please," Zenobia asked while Callie was, "I'll have a white wine. Thank you."

"Actually, I was thinking more like Sprite, or Coke?" The woman smiled. "Unless your ID says you're older than you look?"

"I like Sprite!" Callie said and Z agreed, "Sprite is good!"

Meanwhile, poor Penny was buried in thought. She was going to say her goodbyes to her last parent. Not to mention she was convinced miserable Misty had something to do with it. She second guessed her decision not to tell her father about his wife's infidelity for the hundredth time. Maybe he would have left her and wouldn't be on life support.

"We here, ma," Callie said and gripped her hand. "Whenever you ready to talk, we right here."

"Love you guys," Penny said leaned on Zenobia's shoulder while holding Callie's hand. She was just an unplug away from them being all she had left.

"Love you too!" they assured her.

CHAPTER EIGHTEEN

*T*he girls landed at LAX and looked around. Everyone was moving quickly like they knew what they were doing while Callie and Zenobia waited to see what happened next. This was Zenobia's first time out of her hometown while the second for Callie.

"Penelope! Oh my god. I'm so sorry!" Sarah was saying when she rushed Penny. Until she saw her hands wrapped in black hands of the black girls on each side. "Who are they?"

"Callie and Zenobia," she replied softly. Soft enough for her to wipe the disdain off of her face.

"Are they with you?" the prissy little bigot asked and scrunched her face even more.

"Yes! These are my friends! Now, can I go see my dad or you have more questions?" Penny snapped. She was on the verge of regretting calling her to meet her at the airport.

Callie and Z were ready to beat her up right there in the terminal but refrained. Both were proud of how she stood up for them. They held her hand all the way out to where a limo waited. The two black girls shared a knowing glance at knowing the girl wasn't as poor as she pretended.

That truth was just another thing weighing heavy on the girl. She had long moved past thinking they would use her for her money. She just wanted to be just the same as everyone else. Little did she know someone else had that same desire for her.

"Family only," a nurse advised when they reached the hospital.

"They are my family," Penny replied quickly.

"I know. Just immediate family inside now," she said softly. "You ladies can have a seat in the waiting room.".

"All of us?" Sarah declared like the notion had a bad taste.

"Mm-mm, no," Zenobia said and shook her head before Callie slapped that taste out of her mouth.

"Yeah, cuz I will. Mm-mm!" Callie said and pressed her lips together to keep the threats and curses from spewing out like lava. Sarah sat across the room and watched them so they couldn't steal the TV.

"Oh my gosh! Penelope!" Misty gushed and rushed over to hug Penny when she stepped into the room.

"Bruh..." Penny said and pried out of her grip. They weren't close enough to be this close, so she wiggled away. Her knees buckled when she looked over at her bedridden father. His chest lifted and fell in unison with one of the machines.

"I'll let you say your goodbye," Misty muttered and eased out of the room. She looked left and right like she was crossing the street. Except she was looking for the doctor she had been flirting with while her husband lay comatose.

"Hey." Penny sighed but refused to cry. She cried a river when her mother died, and it didn't help. Instead, she nodded with the advice he used to give. "I got this! I got you. I'm going to finish my degree and make you proud..."

Penny was having her last words while Misty caught up to the doctor at a vending machine. She overlooked the yellow girl buying soda to shoot her shot at the doctor.

"Well, hello again!" Misty sang and twirled her hair in her finger. "Remember me?"

"Of course. I'm your husband's doctor," he squinted to see what she was getting at.

"Soon to be ex-husband. We're pulling the plug today," she said. "What you doing later?"

"Everything that has nothing to do with you," he said and walked off. Misty stood there blinking as her mind processed the dis. The fog of pills, weed and alcohol slowed that process to a crawl.

"Dang." Zenobia laughed and took the sodas back for her and Callie.

"Tuh!" Misty huffed and marched back to the room. She was ready to snatch the plug out the wall herself so she could go home.

"Are we ready?" the same doctor from the hallway asked but only to Penny. The words were too heavy to speak so she just nodded.

The doctor in turn nodded to the nurse who began turning the life support systems off. They don't literally pull the plug so much as just power the machines down. Penny held onto her father's hand while his wife stood across the room. This was the day Misty had planned for when she married the older man.

"Goodbye, father," she said when the man gave her a hand a squeeze and went limp.

"Y'all need me to sign anything?" Misty said, turning towards the door.

"Actually, yes," the doctor said, slowing her escape. She was the wife which meant signing for the death certificate and possession of the empty shell.

"Are you staying at my house?" Misty asked as Penny left the room.

"No, I'm staying at my house," she replied over her shoulder and disappeared.

"We'll see whose house real soon," she muttered.

"I'm so sorry!" Callie pouted and rushed over to Penny when she appeared in the waiting room. Zenobia came over and made it a group hug while Sarah looked on.

"Come on. I'll take you home," Sarah announced. "We can drop your friends off in Compton, or Watts, or wherever."

"Dassit, Zenobia growled but this time it was Callie who saved Sarah from the ass kicking she was campaigning for.

"They're coming with me." Penny sighed. They loaded back into the waiting limo and made a quiet, uncomfortable ride to the house.

"Call me," Sarah said when they arrived at the mansion. She nodded and got out when they reached the gate. Zenobia and Callie weren't sure what to do, so they didn't budge.

"We're here," Penny called as the driver retrieved their bags from the trunk.

"Here where?" is what Callie needed to know while Zenobia asked, "Who stays here?"

"Um, I do?" she answered unsurely. It sure looked like the house, but she didn't know any of the people milling about. Even the people who pulled up in her car.

"Sup," the guy nodded and headed inside with a fresh case of beer.

"What the—" she wondered aloud, then went crazy. "Give me my damn keys!"

"That's your car? This is your house?" her friends asked

again as they followed her inside. Twenty more people were laid out on sofas, chairs and the stairs. Beer bottles, cigarette butts and blunt clips littered the marble floors.

"Excuse me! Excuse me!" Penny called as she turned off the stereo. Once she had half of their attention she ordered, "Everyone get the fuck out of my house!"

"Y'all heard her! Out!" Z and Callie cosigned and started ushering people towards the front door.

"What the hell is going on down here?" a man demanded as he came down the stairs.

"Oh hell naw!" P-money growled when she made her appearance. She recognized the man and her father's robe at the same time he recognized her.

"Oh. Hey, Penny!" Greg cheered as if him being in her house, in her father's robe was something to cheer about.

"Take off my father's robe, and get the fuck out of my house!" she growled and balled her fist. Friends may not let friends drink and drive, but they did ball their fists along with her.

"I'm Misty's guest so..." he shrugged smugly. Callie and Zenobia were ready to fight but she had a better idea.

"I'm calling the police!" Penny said and pulled her phone. This was Brentwood, so a cop was on the line as soon as she dialed 911..

"Brentwood Police Department. I've dispatched three units to your location. How can I help you?" the dispatcher asked.

"Uh-oh," Greg said and pulled the robe off. The trio of friends peeped at his dick before he rushed back upstairs to dress.

"Bruh, it takes two weeks for the cops to come in Harlem!" Callie said as the first cop knocked on the door in under a minute.

"Show me your hands!" the cops demanded and pulled their weapons on the two black girls. Never mind the twenty white folks running around. All they saw was black.

"They're with me! Everyone else needs to go!" Penny declared and put herself between the guns and her friends. Something both of them noticed and would never forget. The cops went room to room clearing freeloaders and squatters. Some had been there the last few months Penny was away at school. One even forwarded his mail there.

"Um..." Callie hummed once the house was finally cleared.

"Okay, so..." Penny began and told her life story. It started with the silver spoon and finished with her arrival at FFF. There was laughter and tears, but by the time the story reached the present, they were all mad. Mad as hell, waiting for Misty to bring her nasty ass in the house.

❧

"*H*ey y'all! Where's everyone at?" Misty asked casually as if the mansion was supposed to be filled with junkies and freeloaders.

"A better question is, why were they here? While my dad was laying in the hospital on his deathbed!'" Penny asked calmly. She was the only calm one because Callie and Zenobia were ready to fight.

"They are my friends and this is my house, in case you forgot?" Misty shot back since she was ready to fight as well.

"Chill," Penny urged when her friends stood. "Once the estate is settled her ass is history."

"Tuh!" Misty huffed and smirked at her back as she walked off. There had been some changes to the will that she didn't know about. Mr. Manning didn't know about them either.

"I need to clear my head," Penny explained as she picked through her bikinis and bathing suites. "Pick something."

"Okay, first of all. All this ass ain't gonna fit none of them!" Callie declared and gave her ass a slap.

"Well, let me see what you talmbout," Zenobia said since she and Penny were closer in size. She walked into the walk-in closet and swooned. "Yo, B. Check this out!"

"What?' Callie asked and came to see. "Damn, chile! You playing poor white girl and got a damn department store in your bedroom!"

"If you see anything you want..." Penny offered and headed to the bathroom to change into a two piece bikini.

"I'm good," Callie decided after perusing the racks of clothes and rows of shows. She liked the finer things in life but wanted to get them on her own.

"Me too," Zenobia said for the same reason except for the red bikini she grabbed and went to find another bathroom to change.

"That bitch!" Penny grumbled when they reached the cluttered pool area. The nonstop party left the water cluttered with debris. Beer cans floated on top while the bottles sank to the bottom.

"Ewww!" Zenobia shrieked when she saw a condom float by. It was just one of many that littered the pool area.

"Yeah," Penny said and stretched out on a lawn chair. She closed her eyes and began to soak in the sun. Callie nodded in approval of her attitude. She had bigger concerns than a dirty pool. She realized then that money didn't insulate people from problems.

"You might wanna join her cuz you looking a lil pale too shawty," Callie teased. Zenobia shot her a bird but still flipped a lawn chair over to clear the trash, then joined her under the rays.

Callie was already a nice, even brown tone, so she went back into the house to explore. The mansion was as cluttered as the pool area. Misty knew her husband wasn't coming home so the party raged on.

"Sup," Misty greeted when Callie's tour reached the study. It was once Mr. Manning's sanctuary until she took it over. The pipe smoke was replaced by the bong she was smoking.

"My friend thinks you had something to do with her dad's death is what's up," Callie dared but Misty didn't deny it. She just shrugged and took another hit from the pipe.

"Yeah, well she'll be alright. When are you guys going back?" she said while exhaling a plume of smoke. "I need to get laid."

"She definitely gonna be good!" Callie snapped and stormed off before she attacked. She knew this was going to be trouble, so she marched back out to the pool. "When are we going back to Atlanta?"

"After I talk to Mr. Haskel. My dad's lawyer," Penny said without opening her eyes. By the time they went back into the house, she had a nice golden tan while Zenobia was still yellow.

CHAPTER NINETEEN

"*Hello*, Penelope!" Mr. Haskel's secretary announced and rushed over to hug Penny as she and her friends walked into the office after the funeral. Mr. Manning was well loved in life so friends, acquaintances and business associates came to show their respects. Including longtime family lawyer Marvin Haskel.

"Hey, Mrs. Alexander," she said and sighed as the woman squeezed her. Penny was handling her dad's death as well as she could, but all the condolences set her back. His being in a coma for months while not expected to survive, served to soften the blow. Now she just missed the goofy man with the heart of gold.

"Penelope," Mr. Haskel greeted as he stepped out of his office. The two black girls stole his attention as he spoke. Only because he loved young black girls. He saw them at the funeral but didn't get to gawk since his wife was on his hip.

"Hello, Mr. Haskel," she replied and followed him into his office. Penny had wanted her friends to come with her, but they took a seat on the sofa and picked up magazines. This was personal so they would let her handle it personally.

"We have a problem. A few problems in fact," he admitted before they both got seated well.

"Of course," Penny said and twisted her lips. "Bet I can guess who."

"Your dad's 'wife'," he began and made quotation marks with his fingers. "Hired another lawyer of her own."

"But you've been with us since..." Penny began and paused to remember when.

"Since before you were born," he helped. "That's why she found some charlatan to change the will."

"Bet she cut my inheritance in half," Penny guessed. It was a good guess even if it was wrong.

"No, she cut you completely out of the estate! Along with all the charitable contributions he set up," he replied. He had set up the continuing charities that would continue helping people long after he was gone. Even if he was gone too soon.

"Can you fix it?" she wondered calmly.

"I can but it won't be quick. It won't be easy. I've already contested it so nothing gets paid out until it's settled," he explained with his mouth but had a 'but' etched into her face.

"But?" she asked of that but.

"But it can take months. Years maybe," he admitted. "How are you for cash?"

"I don't know?" she asked since she was used to the bottomless well that her dad supplied her with. She pulled her account up on her phone and twisted her lips at the amount. "Ten thousand dollars."

"Okay. If you need anything, you let me know," Mr. Haskel sighed.

"What about my house? Can I kick her out?" Penny

inquired. All she needed was the legal nod and her and her crew would go toss her out on her ear.

"No. In fact, it's her legal place of residence. She could ask you to leave if she wanted to," he regrettably informed.

"What am I supposed to do now?" she asked with her lip quivering on the verge of tears.

"Nothing you can do. Go back to school. Focus on your grades and I'll handle this mess," he assured her.

Penny literally willed the tears not to come. She was a pretty thug and pretty thugs don't cry. She hopped to her feet and extended her hand across the desk as she had seen her dad do plenty of times throughout the years. Mr. Haskel nodded and shook her hand.

"If you need anything..." he repeated to her back as she walked out of the office.

"Err thing good?" Zenobia asked since nothing was written on her face.

"It will be," she said and led the way back to her car. Penny was deep in thought as she drove back to the house. By the time they arrived, she had made up her mind. Now it was time to put those plans in motion.

"So, what now?" Callie asked when they arrived back at the house.

"Now you better get what you want from that closet. Good Will is coming for the rest!" she said and called the pickup line for the charity. Callie and Zenobia declined so the underprivileged could get it all.

"Except this," Callie said and claimed a designer purse.

"Well, this too," Zenobia said and collected one for herself. That set off a slight shopping spree since she was giving it all away anyway. "Poor people don't need Prada."

Next step was calling an auto transport company to ship

her car back east since she wasn't up for driving it across the country. She booked the cheapest flights she could find but was still down over half of the ten thousand dollars she had left. Mr. Haskel's promise was promising, but she didn't plan on using it.

Her late mother often told her stories of being poor and thuggin' her way through college. Her parents were poor when they met and built an empire. She was their kid and determined to make it too.

"One more thing," Penny said and hopped up the steps. Callie and Zenobia wondered what she was doing since Misty wasn't in the house. She returned a few minutes later holding a bag of pills. More than enough to replace the money she just spent. "Let's go back to school!"

❦

"We need to party?" Penny asked because she wasn't quite sure how else to move the pills. Plus, she had just buried her father right next to her mother which doubled the depression. Sitting around the dorm room certainly wasn't helping.

"We should," Zenobia agreed quickly since she knew the pain of burying a parent. Hers was multiplied by thinking she was the cause of her mother's death.

"I'm down," Callie agreed in support. She was the only one who never met either parent which was a pain of itself.

Penny rushed into the bathroom to shower first. Callie would be next since Zenobia always took the longest. The three had synced all the way down to their cycles. They moved in harmony until three baddies set out to turn the party out. The Benz had just arrived, but they still hoofed it over.

A local fraternity was having it's Thanksgiving party but they found any reason to party. The frat house was in walking distance, so they walked. That meant turning down rides and offers to be walked the whole way over.

"Look what we have here! Not the mean girls!" A male student laughed. The girls were dubbed mean since they weren't fucking. Sleeping around must be nice, but Penny was quick to set the record straight.

"Naw, B. Pretty thugs up in here!" She barked back.

"B?" Zenobia laughed.

"She always says it," Penny said, nodding at Callie. Her face scrunched and she asked, "Why B?"

"Before my time, yo," she said and shrugged as they entered the party. It may have been dimly lit inside, but the men saw the new meat.

Dudes saw the girls on campus all the time, but this was the first time they saw them at a party and came running. Especially for the white girl.

"Dang!" Callie fussed when she was nearly run down by dudes trying to get to Penny. That's when she noticed Penny turned into P-money as a defense mechanism.

"Chill! Why you all up on me!" she fussed and controlled the crowd. "Y'all must be tryna shop?"

"P-money," Callie laughed as students lined up to purchase the pills. They sold out the supply they brought in no time.

"Let's hit this dance floor!" Zenobia demanded when the DJ mixed in the latest Erv-G banger on.

The trio had spent most of the semester dancing in their dorm room, so it was only right that they had developed a routine, or two. More like twenty but they only showed off one for the night. All the guys loved it but only half the women. Not because it wasn't good, they just hadn't learned how to celebrate other people's accomplishments.

"Pretty thugs, tuh!" one chick hissed as the crowd cheered them on. She wasn't happy until the song wrapped up and they relinquished the dancefloor.

"Pretty thugs out!" Callie announced and led the way to the exit.

"Y'all wanna get some breakfast?" the spokesman of the three men who reached them first asked, while the other practically posed to show off their good looks.

"We sure do!" Zenobia cheered but it was a set up.

"By ourselves, tho!" Penny quipped and left them standing.

A local hustler took advantage of the late-night crowds and set up a food trailer. It wasn't registered with the health department but still clean and served good food. Perfect for late night, after the party people.

The girls ordered burgers and fries since they were still young even to get away with all those carbs. They happily cackled their way back to the dorm but didn't make it. They were a block away when someone jumped out with a gun.

"Y'all bitches know what it is!" a familiar voice announced. The girls all squinted as they tried to place the face. It was Zenobia who saw the grit and grime first.

"Michaela? You really finna rob us?" she dared and Michaela fired a shot into the air as a reply.

"Oh, okay. Here you go. Take it!" the girls said as they broke off themselves. Penny even parted with the hundreds they made off the pills. They still had plenty left, so it didn't make sense dying over.

"Go on, yo!" Callie demanded once she had taken their money. Michaela still pointed the gun between the three instead of running off.

"Naw, y'all hoes dissed me!" Michaela growled and moved

the gun back and forth at their faces. "Eenie, meenie, minie, mo. One of y'all hoes gots ta go."

A single shot rang out in the cool night air and one person dropped dead.

The End

Stay tuned for Pretty Thugs 2. In the meanwhile, check out the new book by Paige Turner...

Creeping with
My
Mama's Man

Paige Turner

oriah woke up out of her sleep to moans being heard through the wall. She tried to put the pillow over her head to tune them out, but it was no use. She guessed that her mama had a new man and from the sounds of things he was pleasing her well.

"Maybe she'll finally stop bitching so much," she mumbled to herself. "All she needs is some good dick!"

The dick sure sounded good because the moans got louder. Soon she heard the headboard starting slamming up against the wall.

"Take this dick, Lynn! Don't run from it! Take daddy's dick!" he grunted and pounded.

"Give it me!" my mama shouted back.

"Throw it back, mama." She laughed to herself. She hoped hope she her mother didn't punk out off some dick.

Moriah shook her head. She couldn't believe that this shit was happening right now. How was she supposed to make it to class in the morning and on time if they were going at it like rabbits? Soon after, her prayers were answered, and she heard some more grunts and screams before the room went silent.

"Finally," she mumbled to herself as she got out of bed and walked to the bathroom. She relieved herself and washed her hands and when she opened the door, she saw the finest man she had ever seen in her life standing beside the door. He stood at least six foot, four inches tall and his hair was cut in a fade.

Moriah almost got stuck on his handsome face and ducked. Only to see the most muscular chests she had ever seen on a man in person. She lowered my gaze a little more but there was a long lump of disk bulging in his pajama pants.

"You must be Lynn's daughter, Moriah," he said when my eyes came back up.

"Yes, I am. I see that you know my name, but I don't have the pleasure in knowing what yours is." She nodded her head.

"My name is Micah," he said. "Did your mom and I wake you up?"

"Yeah, a little bit and I kind of have class in the morning so I better be getting back to sleep." She peeped the small smirk that he had on his face. "Well, I guess I'll see you in the morning." he said with that same smirk.

She nodded her head and walked past him. When she did she felt his dick brush across her arm. She didn't know if it was intentional or not, so she shrugged it off and walked back to her room. She laid back in the bed and tried to fall back asleep but after five minutes, the moans in her mom's room started back up. After laying eyes on him herself, she saw why her mom would be anxious to climb back on top of that man. Hell, she would be to. She picked up her iPhone and placed in her headphones. She played music and fell asleep to the sounds of Beyoncé and the thought of Micah dicking her down the way that he was doing to her mother.

CHAPTER ONE

$\mathcal{M}$oriah woke up the next morning to her alarm blaring in her ear. She was able to at least get a few hours of sleep after she was able to tune out her mom's fuck session from the night before. She hopped out of the bed and flipped through her closet to see what she was going to wear to class today.

She only had a few more months left in college so to save money she was staying here with her mom until she graduated. She picked out a pair of black ripped jeans and a tight, white shirt. She then got dressed, brushed her teeth and headed downstairs. She didn't hear anyone's voice, just the sound of breakfast being cooked so she assumed that her mom had to be in there.

"Hey, mom. What smells good," she said as she took a seat but was surprised to see no other than Micah standing over the stove cooking up breakfast. "My bad. I thought that my mom was in here."

"No need for you to apologize. Your mom left earlier because they called her into work." He smiled.

"And she just left you here by yourself?" she asked with a raised brow.

"No, you're here so I'm not alone. And in a little while I will be going to work myself," he said. "Do you want some food?"

"That depends. What did you cook?" she asked a little too sassy.

"I cooked some French toast, bacon, and a Philly cheesesteak omelet," he said like he was proud of himself.

"Sure, I'll take some," she said as she walked to fridge and fixed herself a glass of orange juice. She couldn't help but check out how tight his shirt fit on him and the thought of seducing him right there on the kitchen table flashed through her mind.

She sat back down at the table, and he placed the food in front of her and it smelled delicious. She was glad that she had agreed to take some. He sat a plate down for himself and sat across from her with a smile on his face.

"So how did you sleep last night?" he asked.

She looked at him and saw a look in his eyes that she just couldn't place. "I put my headphones in because I couldn't sleep because you and my mom insisted on making so much noise. After that, I slept fine."

He chuckled. "Well, your mom is a wild woman. It was a little hard to keep her off of me but I'm sorry that we kept you up. We'll try to be a little quieter next time."

"That was a little more information than I needed to know, but okay thanks," she said as she took a bite of the omelet. "Oh my gosh! This taste so good. Definitely better than the one at Waffle House."

"Yeah, well I try," he said. "I'm glad that you enjoy it."

"So where do you work? You don't look as if you're going to an office." Moriah asked after checking him out once more.

"I'm not. I'm a personal trainer. I work at a gym." he replied, again like he was proud of himself.

"Oh really? Which one?" she asked as if she knew about more than the one the athletes from her school used.

"The new one by your college." Micah nodded.

She raised her brow. "How do you know where I go to school?"

"Your mother told me on our first date. She talked about you a lot. She's very proud of you. I hope that you know that." He nodded.

"Yeah, I know that she's proud of me. I know that she'll probably be even happier once I graduate and get out of her hair and then you two can be as loud as you want," she said with a smirk.

"Maybe," he said as he stared her down. The look that he gave her sent chills down her spine and she felt a little tingle in between her legs.

"So, I've been thinking about getting in shape. You know toning my body up a little. You think that you could train me?" Moriah asked.

"I think so. Come in this afternoon and I could give you a trial session," he said as he stood up from the table and placed his dishes in the sink.

"Okay, I'll do that. Anything in particular I'll need?"

"Just some comfortable clothes and shoes," he said. "Well, I'm about to head out because I have a client meeting me in about an hour. I'll see you this afternoon."

"You sure will," she said.

He smiled at her and let his gaze go over her body one more time before he walked out of the kitchen and then out of the house. She licked her lips as she took another bite of the omelet.

"Damn, that man knows he know how to make a woman

wet," she said to herself. She finished the food and the juice, grabbed her keys and headed out of the door. She couldn't wait until this afternoon to see what Mr. Micah was all about.

After a long three hours of classes, Moriah walked out of the classroom with her best friend, Laysia.

"I'm telling you, girl. He's so fine. Him and my mom were in there fucking all night long. I couldn't even sleep. Sounded like that nigga was trying to push her head through the headboard or some shit," she said.

"Girl, stop! Don't tell me your mama got her groove back." Laysia laughed.

"Shit, last night she got her groove back enough for me and you," she laughed.

"So did you know yo mama had a new man?" her friend asked.

"No girl. I thought my mama been bout to be a spinster or some shit. I haven't seen her with anyone since her and my dad split a few years back. And she been snappy so I knew she wasn't getting any."

"Shit, well I guess Mr. Micah knocked the cobwebs off that pussy." she laughed loudly, causing Moriah to crack up as well.

"Man, shut up girl. You stupid. What you about to get into?"

"Well, I got another class in about thirty minutes so probably going to grab me something out of the cafeteria and then head there. What you about to do?" she replied.

"I don't know. Probably head home and take a nap and then go to the gym and see Micah." I said innocently.

"You're going to see your mama's man?" Laysia raised her brow.

"It's not that serious girl. He's a personal trainer. He offered me the chance to come and train with him so I'm going to take him up on the offer. Besides, I need to get in shape anyway." she explained.

"Mmm, yeah you do," said Laysia.

"Girl, I'm slim thick with a booty to match," she shot back and dipped her hip as proof.

"Yeah, you do kinda got that coke bottle figure. That pudge could use a little tightening up though," said Laysia with a smirk.

"That's the wine I be drinking because these classes be having me stressed."

"Mm hmm, and the burgers that you be eating and all the other fast food that you push down your throat." Laysia laughed

"I know you not talking Ms. Hot Wing queen." Moriah laughed.

"Yeah, you right. I may need to get my ass in the gym too. But I'm too lazy. Besides, these niggas be eating me up just like this!"

"They do," she said and twisted her lips since she didn't get as much attention. "But I know I want to try it out at least this one time. I might like it. If not, then well at least I built up a sweat with a fine ass man."

"Mmhmm. I know you been eyeing Ms. Lynn man," Laysia said and shook her head again.

"Nah, she can have him but there's nothing wrong with looking right?"

"Yeah, nothing is wrong with looking as long as you don't touch. Especially since he might be your daddy one day!" she said seriously.

"Don't worry. I won't be touching a thing." Moriah vowed and crossed her heart even though that dick print came to mind. Plus, she wasn't even Catholic.

CHAPTER TWO

"You don't like me don't you," said Moriah as she felt the burn in her legs from doing twenty-five squats.

Micah laughed. "No, I'm not trying to kill you and you've only been doing this for twenty minutes. Most sessions take one to two hours and to top it off I'm going easy on you. I know that you can do better than this."

She shot him a look as if he were crazy. Her legs were burning and she felt as if her chest was about to cave in at any second. This was going to be her first and last time in the gym. It wasn't for her at all. She didn't know how all those gym fanatics pulled it off.

"Nah, I don't think that I will be training. My body isn't built for this. I commend your other clients for doing this because I'd pass out a long time ago. And people really do this for an hour?" Moriah asked sincerely.

"Some do it longer than an hour," he said as he leaned against one of the machines.

"Yeah, I tip my hat to them," she said as she sat down on the floor and tried to catch her breath.

"Here, drink this," he said as he handed her a bottle of water. "This will help you feel a little better. Just try not to gulp it."

She grabbed the water bottle and completely ignored what he said. She drank that water as if it were the first drink she had ever had in her life. "That hit the spot."

"Just ignored what I said huh?" Micah laughed musically.

"Sorry, but a sister needed that." Moriah apologized. He just smiled and shook his head.

"Well lay back while I help you stretch out. You're going to be in a lot of pain for about a day or two because your body will have to adjust to your muscles being worked so much. You would've gotten used to it if you decided to keep on training, but I don't think that there's any changing your mind." He sighed.

"Nope. Not interested. I'm not about the gym life," she laughed seriously.

"Okay, well lay flat on your back so that I can stretch your legs out for you." Micah directed.

She laid back on her back and looked up at him. He hadn't even broken into a sweat since they began training thirty minutes ago and the front of her shirt was completely drenched in sweat, and she could only imagine how her hair looked. It didn't matter though. He probably saw women looking busted all the time in his line of work. He grabbed a hold of one of her legs and lifted it in the air and pushed it back a little.

"How does that feel?" he asked as he continued to stretch out her leg.

"It doesn't feel too bad. It's helping with a little bit of the soreness," she said. I'm so glad I'm wearing black shorts because I know that I'm getting really wet in between my thighs, she thought to herself.

"Yeah, it definitely helps out a lot. I try to stretch all of my new clients out, so they won't cramp up later on," he said. "If you want, I can give you a massage after this too."

She looked at him and wondered if that had any hidden meaning in it. She knew that he had to been flirting with her earlier this morning, and maybe some last night. Or maybe he was just that friendly. Either way, at the moment she didn't want to place herself in a predicament where she was going to be unsure of herself and her actions.

"No, I'm okay. You don't need to massage me. I'll just go home and take a long shower or soak in the tub."

"Okay, if that's what you really want." Micah laughed knowingly.

"Yeah, it is. Although I may take you up on that offer some other time," she said. "I gotta go now. I have this paper that I need to get started on for class."

"Okay, well I guess I'll see you later," he said.

"I'm sure you will," she said since he was dating or fucking her mama.

Visit www.prettythugs.net for official Pretty Thugs merchandise.

CPSIA information can be obtained
at www.ICGtesting.com
Printed in the USA
LVHW020344010322
712223LV00015B/2504